Dropping Out:

The Trespasser Killer

By Ned Johnson

Dedication:

This book is dedicated to anyone who ever thought of

cashing in their chips and saying goodbye to humanity by

finding their piece of a place like Hank's Heaven.

Chapter One...Money Doesn't Buy Happiness, But It Solves Problems

I am done...Done my thing for President and country...time for me...

With a determined hand, and heart to match, Conrad Nevitt began the laborious process of signing and initialing document after document. A smile traced his lips each time initials were made, the bright green C-A-N letters illuminating the stiffly written document. A few more pages and life would never be the same.

Not that he wanted the same – this was exactly the purpose for all of this paperwork – one last reminder of the world he decided to leave behind – a world no longer meant for someone who once cared about everyone.

@#!! 'em!

The last page presented itself and after one last set of initials, the full signature ended the process.

"Congratulations, Mr. Nevitt, Hank's Heaven is now all yours."

Mr's Ass, I've known this bank lady all her life and she's calling me Mr. Of course, this is probably the hardest work she's done all day or all week or all year. Oh, except the time she bragged about putting a recipe book together of the bank people's favorite dishes. Never have I been in here when there weren't four or five people standing around gossiping about this person's finances or that person's bankruptcy or...hell, they should have customer/teller confidentiality like doctors or lawyers, but then these people wouldn't have anything to talk about.

He continued to amuse himself with thoughts of how little these people actually did for the salaries received yet how self-important all believed themselves to be. Perhaps these people represented a microcosm of the country, bathed in delusionment about their places in the universe. Technology replaced them long ago, but banks enjoyed enough profits at the expense of their customers that they could keep people around as a sign of "the personal touch".

They should take a hypocritic oath...

As Miss Self-Important took the papers for the purpose of frivolously murdering another tree, Conrad fought against the last vestiges of sadness at the decision made, content with knowing this was the best decision for him – one of the first times in his life a decision was made solely with him in mind. He was no saint, and the mere thought of St. Conrad nearly caused an audible laugh. Named after Brother Conrad, last headmaster of St. Xavier School and a Xaverian clergyman, he lived his life as he was raised: to be everything to everyone with no thought to the consequences to self. The life was solid but turned negative through a horrible series of choices he'd made trying to help people – people who, simply put, were no damned good. They were parasites – leeches of the first order, and they drained him of everything good except in one area – this decision to leave the world behind.

"Sorry it took so long, Mr. Nevitt. The copier is so slow these days."

Excuses...he'd heard enough excuses from people to last a lifetime; actually, the excuses nearly took his lifetime, so one more only served as more evidence he was doing the right thing. Everything he had was going into this purchase with as many ties cut as humanly possible. When the property became his, the only contact with the outside world would be in three venues: cyberspace, Wal-Mart and Direct TV. He would succeed in doing what the late, great philosopher George Carlin wanted to do: sit back and watch the world go to hell. George wasn't ahead of his time – he was on time.

Conrad took the papers.

"Congratulations, Mr. Nevitt, I hope you are happy on your new property. If there is anything we can ever do for you, please do not hesitate to contact us."

Nodding as if he cared about the bullshit uttered, he walked out of the bank, a free man perhaps for the first time in his life. Anxious to get on with his flee from humanity, he became nearly giddy moving toward his SUV. Ironically, his former best friend, Boone Bowling, was standing at the car.

"Congratulations Con! Can't wait to see the place once you fix it up."

"Won't be fixing it up, Boone, and there will be no company. All trespassers will be shot."

Conrad amazed himself at the calmness in his voice.

"What? Oh, hell, Con, you're not serious with all that talk about getting away from it all. We know you – you can't be without people for long."

"Sounds like a challenge...always loved a good challenge. Spread the word, Boone, and we'll see who the first person is that gets shot. Make sure it's not you."

"You are serious."

"Good-bye, Boone, and make sure you do what I told you. I sent letters to the sheriff and the police chief letting them know my intention – did my homework. According to the laws of this state, if I apprise the sheriff and police chief, and put up the proper signs, I can shoot anyone coming onto my property."

"Never known you to shoot a gun."

"Took a course last year when I made this decision. As long as people leave me alone, no one will get hurt. Anyone disobeys, they will be shot. By the way, you might spread that I aced that course and can put out a candle at 300 yards. Never knew I had the proficiency. Probably a good thing for some people that I didn't use it."

"I don't know what to say."

"Nothing to say…You were a good friend most of the time, except for times you weren't. Live a good life and maybe we'll see each other in the next journey."

"Hope you don't take a gun with you."

"Good joke to end on. Good-bye, Boone, and again, make sure you do what I told you."

Boone nodded, but Conrad could tell he wasn't convinced. Hope was he didn't find out the hard way that intentions were indeed to shoot anyone coming on his property – anyone. He would change if the law changed, but the NRA would never let politicians change this law, and finally, he was going to use the law to his advantage. People in his life had used laws against him, and he was done with that and them.

Conrad climbed into the seat and shut the door. Easing out of the parking lot, thoughts drifted to the multitude of things achieved and the multitude of things left undone. Still, he was satisfied with how he had come to this point – this decision – and he was ready for the final chapter. Sixty-two years old and in relatively good health for a 62 year-old man, he stopped at the city limits, just past a sign that read: Voted Best City in America!

The sad news was they (whomever they are...) were probably right. All the more a pity...if this was the best of America, the so-called land of the free was no more. All the more evidence to substantiate what his next step in life had to be.

Conrad Nevitt drove 12 miles to the middle of nowhere, and the final adventure began.

Chapter 2...Remembrance

As the lock on the second gate clicked behind him, Conrad let out a banshee scream:

"AWWWWWWWWWWWWWWWWWWSHHHHHHHEEEEEEEEEEEEEEEEEEYIT!"

Done...over...no more society. He wondered often how this would feel when the moment came – wondered often if the moment would come. Now time and good (or bad) fortune brought him to this point. How did he feel?

Revelatory! He remembered an old English professor's definition of love: "Love is revelation." A profound influence on his high school mind, Conrad remembered fondly Mr. Curney, a spit-and-polish grammarian and stickler for all rules except one in writing. He never believed in limits, constraints, and censorship.

Department of redundancy department, he mused, thinking of one of the corrective measures Mr. Curney used to write on papers. He caught himself often in internal thought grammatical mistakes, and amused himself when feeling the need to correct himself in a world no one was allowed. He thought of the thousands of corrected papers for students, the countless marks in green ink rather than red (green more apt to be read than red), and the countless funny juxtapositions: "Carpet Diem" (seize the rug or carpet the day) jumped into his mind first, as it always did.

Back to reality, Conrad climbed back into the vehicle and moved toward the two dwellings on what was now HIS land. He could choose to live in one or the other, or go back and forth between the two. Each possessed charm: an A-frame structure built by his grandfather and great-uncle Hank, or a cabin overlooking a small pond. The A-frame enjoyed more basics, with indoor plumbing, including a shower, plus a loft that could be a bedroom or a writer's garret. The cabin enjoyed more rusticity, with a still-working fireplace and panoramic views from each window. No indoor plumbing with the cabin, but an outhouse a few yards away served its purpose.

No decision required today; in fact, no decision anytime. He owned both, so both were now home. In the back of his mind, there was a plan; in the back of his mind, there was always a plan even though most people thought he lived his life without one. All of his life, his plan was to be here at this point in time. His dream, even as a young boy, was to eventually own this place and live on it. Granted, as a young boy, he thought it would provide an oasis for all of his friends and family to visit and enjoy – his vision then was of family and friends constantly being around, laughing, hiking, fishing, picnicking, singing, telling jokes, and basking in the comraderie that made Hank's Heaven his favorite place on earth.

Now, while Hank's Heaven remained his favorite place on earth, time taught him to share it with no one. The people he cherished were either dead, and more cherished than ever, or alive and semi-well living in their own delusion. Those people who let him down time after time, still could not believe he could separate from them – could not believe he could cut them out of his life. They miscalculated their value, although, if they simply played their cards correctly, that value would remain. As with most of humanity, they took and they took and they took until he was tired of giving.

They never counted on him ever tiring. The irony realized in each of them became absurd. If they simply begat honesty with him, and told him they simply wanted to use him, he would have been fine with that; however, lying to him about their constant use of his talents and then showing little to no appreciation of all he gave finally broke him of his need for people in general...and them in particular.

Conrad Nevitt smiled as he broke the train of thought.

Told yourself you weren't going to get bogged down in that...this is a new day – your day. Thinking of all of your mistakes regarding people will only serve to tear yourself down...they did a superb job of that for a long time. It's YOUR time now, Conrad, and put them out of your head and enjoy what God gave you: a decent mind, decent health, decent retirement, and this place you love more than any on earth.

The original question re-entered: the A-frame or the cabin. Since the middle of summer approached, and the air conditioner in the A-frame was brand new, the answer seemed simple on the surface. Plus, it was nearer the gates and a bit lower in elevation than the cabin, with a true yard surrounding it. Anyone coming near the A-frame would be easily spotted – someone coming to the cabin could use brush, trees, and two hillsides to cover the approach. Conrad continued to weigh pros and cons, and neither dwelling seemed superior to the other. He loved them both, so he would use them both. Was inside temperature the defining factor? But heat never bothered Conrad, and the cabin was surrounded by pine trees as old as the hills, nature's air conditioning at work. The cabin never seemed to be too hot or too cold, and its window air conditioning unit lived a life like many people formerly in Conrad's life: little work.

He remembered when his grandfather put the unit in, but only remembered a time or two it had been on. It wasn't even new then, having been a window unit at his grandfather's house for several years before making the switch.

Guess it retired long before me, but nothing wrong with coming out of retirement from time to time. Might do it myself. Never say never...oops, just did.

Conrad remembered the several weekends he stayed in the cabin with his grandparents. He smiled at one particular moment, perhaps the funniest unfunny moment ever at Hank's Heaven.

The family was gathered outside the cabin. Conrad couldn't remember the lineup, but remembered there were a number of them listening to his grandfather pontificate on things of the mind and the spirit, as he often did after sneaking some "spirits" compliments of the James B. Beam Distilling Company. Conrad remembered the particular story, one of Panther Pete, a legendary family member who followed Daniel Boone across the Cumberland Gap into Kain-tuck-ee, or at least that was the story. He always considered Panther Pete most intelligent – smart enough to make Daniel Boone go in first!

Conrad smiled and the memory of his grandfather's storytelling ability became vivid as if it happened recently, not fifty years ago:

"Papa, tell us about Panther Pete again..."

"Oh, hell, I've told that story so many times you have to be bored with it."

"Never, Papa, tell us."

"Aight...well, Panther Pete got his name down in the state of Florida when he was doing some trackin' for the gummit who wanted to know what the Seminoles were upto. Now ole Pete had the longest arms you ever did see – seemed like he could scratch his calves without bendin' over. Those long arms made him one of the country's great wrasslers and sure came in handy one night near the Suwanee River. Seems Pete made camp one night with a mate of his named Billy Ray. Now, Pete was a helluva good campfire cook. He'd shot some varmint – don't recall what kind – don't matter, because he could make a possum taste like a t-bone steak with the special spices he brought with him from the old country. Well, he took to cookin' this varmint when, lo and behold, a Florida panther came into his camp, and just set down, eyeballing Pete without one speck of hostility. Pete knew animals better than people, and liked 'em a helluva lot better, so he picked up on the panther not being a danger to him...just wanted to sit by the fire. So Pete and Billy Ray let him be and went about their business, except talkin' to the panther as he cooked. The panther seemed interested in the varmint, so Pete beckoned him to have a bite. Gave him a leg and the panther ate it in a heartbeat. Pete told the panther he could have the other leg but leave the breast the hell alone – that was Pete's favorite part and he didn't share the breast with no livin' creature...even Billy Ray. The panther seemed fine with that, and gobbled the second leg right down. Everything was goin' well until Pete went to cut the breast. The damned panther waited for him to slice off a big piece and then jumped at it and swallowed it whole. The problem came about as Pete's hand and arm were still attached to the breast as it went down the throat of the predator. The two creatures eyeballed each other again, and Pete calmly apprised that the bastard better let go of the breast or dire consequences would result. The panther shook his head left to right and back left again to let

Pete know the breast was not going anywhere. Billy Ray told Pete he might just let the panther have the breast, but that wasn't Pete's way because he'd told the creature what he couldn't do and he'd be damned if he'd let the creature get away with the one thing he told him not to do. Well, don't you know that pissed ole Pete off so much, he reached his arm and shoulder all the way to the panther's tail on the inside, grabbed it, and pulled so hard he pulled that panther inside out. He got his breast back. From then on, he was known throughout the South as Panther Pete. Ole Billy Ray was a storyteller, and would tell it in every tavern south of the Mason-Dixon...and Billy Ray never skipped a tavern! If memory serves me correctly, that man's full name was William Raymond Beam. And that is the story of how Panther Pete got his name.

Conrad laughed out loud in the wilderness, and a tear formed in his right eye with so many good memories of his grandfather. Still, the laughter was not at the Panther Pete story, it's what happened at the end of the telling. He remembered his grandfather rising with pride as he spoke that last line and, as he did, a small, copper-colored snake leaped from the roof of the cabin onto the big man's shoulder. Never before or again Conrad heard such a litany of "colorful metaphors" come from anyone's mouth, and the scene ended with the grandfather leaping off the small hill into the water below. To this day, no one figured out who exhibited more fear at that moment: the grandfather or the snake.

When the grandfather died years later, the snake story was part of the wake, and all enjoyed the memory.

As good as that memory lived, the better ones were of Conrad's grandmother. She adored Hank's Heaven, because she loved fishing, and the three ponds on the property gave her unbridled joy. One never knew how large the fish was that she caught because her laughter rang through the trees like every fish was a trophy, but it might be the tiniest of bluegill. She simply loved seeing the fish. She preferred the cabin to the A-frame, because she could put on a porch light and fish at night. When she was with us, we stayed in the cabin.

Duh! Conrad realized why the A-frame was built in the first place. Grandmother preferred the cabin, so Grandfather built another place for him. A master carpenter who built lots of houses, it took a surprisingly long time for the Grandfather to finish it. The young mind simply believed he was making sure everything was done right. The older mind now realizes he was away from her and both of them enjoyed the time alone. That's why they were married over sixty years.

Once the A-frame was finished, the cabin saw less and less use, because Grandmother double-crossed his plan and stayed in the A-frame. Of course, on third thought, perhaps Grandfather's run-in with the snake caused him to get as far away from the cabin as possible.

Conrad realized no decision needed to be made today. Where he put his bag of clothes today mattered not in the grand scheme of things. Nothing set in stone. These silly decisions were other reasons why he said goodbye to the "real" world to come to this real world. Perhaps an omen could arise. He chuckled at how people look at the world and see omens everywhere. He chuckled at how people put so much emphasis on these omens. He chuckled at how stupid people were.

He perused the A-frame. It seemed to lack personality, other than the loft. Conrad then looked up the small hill to the cabin. Movement. Something fairly large loomed at the cabin's side.

The growl, more inviting than terrorizing, resonated through the pines.

The cabin it was.

Chapter 3...Settling Into Isolation

The large shadow faded into the rear of the cabin as Conrad moved closer. With youthful enthusiasm believed long faded, his pace quickened to a full trot (to call it running would be an insult to runners everywhere). Rounding the back of the building, eyes scanned the hillside directly behind the cabin.

Nothing.

Movement lower right caught his glance. The rows of cattails threatening to overtake the small pond were parting like a thresher was in their midst. Conrad moved to the corner back of the cabin, not forgetting to look up at the roof – a practice invoked since the infamous snake incident with the grandfather. No snakes on the roof were discerned, so Conrad's eyes darted to the hillside that met the end of the cattails on the opposite side of the pond. Emerging was a tan figure larger than any cat he'd seen outside of a zoo. The feline paused, turning its head slightly to meet the stunned gaze of the human 100 yards away separated only by water.

"Are you my omen?"

Conrad smiled at his ignorance, thinking the creature would have any clue what that meant – smiled at the ignorance of humans thinking they were superior to these creatures of the wild who learned to adapt to man's stupidity of the environment. God might have made man caretakers of the earth, but man continuously ignored the instruction manual.

A slight growl emanated from the big cat – not a growl of ferocity or anger, but one that seemed acknowledging Conrad's existence.

"Do we know each other?"

Conrad no longer felt ignorant at talking to a creature he deemed smarter than at least this particular human. However, the big cat bounded up the hillside and out of sight. After pondering whether to follow or not, the decision was made that the forest denizen would have given a sign had he wanted to be followed. No need to tempt fate on the first day.

Strange...I don't feel scared at all. What the hell? I just looked into the eyes of something that could have eaten me for lunch, or at least maimed me for life, and yet there is no fear present. Why not?

Fear certainly held a place in his psyche, having spent a lifetime with one fear or another. Fear of failure, fear of not pleasing people, fear of simply not being good enough, fear of not having enough money, fear of being alone...all legitimate and all a part of him. Of course, he no longer feared being alone; in fact, he savored isolation.

Did that cause all other fears to exit the building? At this point, he knew plenty of time existed to explore the absence of fear...unless, of course, the cat returned for dinner.

Another smile as he pondered whether the cat thought him tasty enough. Perhaps the feline ate a human once upon a time and the subsequent indigestion caused him to avoid them thereafter. The Ron White joke about the man eaten by a grizzly bear came to mind: the man proved his father wrong when the father proclaimed, "You'll never amount to shit!"

Unpacking proved less of a chore than imagined, mainly because most of the clothes brought remained in their bags. No sense in getting out winter clothes in the middle of summer, and since they are already neatly folded, why waste time moving them from the bag to the chest of drawers? His old chest of drawers, delivered here months ago, remained one of his few prized possessions. The chest belonged to a great-grandmother he never knew well, although she lived to be 104. Her secret to longevity? Two shots of 100 proof Jim Beam every day and plenty of herbs added to her diet. Conrad remembered the herb garden but never asked the names of each. He'd brought along seed packets of the herbs planned for a garden should he have one – that decision would come next spring. He probably wouldn't, but liked to keep options open. He hadn't moved here to be a farmer because he knew the best farmer he could hope to emulate was Eddie Albert in *Green Acres*. Immediately, the theme popped into his head – one sung many times to make people laugh…and usually succeeded. It was the one time perhaps he felt the need for Eva Gabor, but that feeling quickly subsided.

No people….at least for the immediate future. Mind-change could happen, but for the immediate future, his vow was to avoid people and to shoot anyone who infringed on that vow. So far, he was making it through today.

The mirror on the top of the chest stared at him. He remembered a time when he wasn't tall enough to look into this mirror and his brother hoisted him.

"See, little brother…ugly as ever!"

"I see two uglies in the mirror."

"No, you see one ugly and one studly."

"But everyone says we look alike, so if I'm ugly, you're ugly too."

"OK, so we're both studly. I can live with that."

"Donnie, what's studly?"

"Something you'll never know about, little brother...it's when women find you irresistible...with your smart mouth, they'll always resist. Now, do you want to get down?"

"Yes."

Always the same last question and always the same result: Donnie dropping him on his posterior and running off with the contagious laugh that permeated the family tree. And as always, sadness streamed through Conrad and the blame game commenced. Try as he might, he couldn't get Donnie to eliminate his demons. Interventions, AA, drug counselors...old loves re-visited...everything tried, nothing worked. Everyone consoled Conrad as a great brother, but in Conrad's heart, a great brother would have succeeded in turning Donnie away from the darkness drugs and alcohol brought. The pity concerned modern medicine's penchant to treat these problems with...more drugs. The things that were prescribed to save Donnie caused him to lose that wonderful mind and caused the nicest human in the universe to go on a killing spree. He was the first convicted murderer in years to actually ask for execution but, of course, the government never gave a person what they wanted. The judge cited how wonderful the family's contributions to society were and "spared" Donnie. That was not mercy, but torture.

Rotting in prison is worse for someone like Donnie who was ready for the next journey. Conrad continued to ponder doing the deed himself, but continued to decide it would not be what his parents would want.

Refrigerator stocked, chest filled, and winter clothes closeted away, Conrad surveyed the cabin. Everything connected. He moved out of the small bedroom into the small living room, past the fireplace and into the small kitchen. Small was good – not much to clutter and obviously an easy cleanup. The cabin's previous owners left the place in solid condition. Conrad ran his hand along the rolltop desk that perched in a corner and took up more space than one piece of furniture should, but that was a good thing as well. Checking his hand, no dust came into view. No cobwebs, even though he remembered cobwebs always being part of this interior. Bugs resided here for decades, but a recent spraying apparently eradicated the insects. For a moment, Conrad felt bad for them, but then remembered an insect bite in this cabin that swelled his left leg to nearly twice its size.

Killing no longer seemed a bad way to go.

He walked again to the rear of the SUV. All that remained were large bags of varmint food. If successful living was the goal, the varmints need to be befriended. Big bowls of various animal delights were arranged in some semblance of order around the cabin, along the dam of the small pond, and even around the A-frame. If he was in the cabin, perhaps the food around the A-frame would be more inviting. He hoped the big cat would return and bring friends.

The cellphone beeped. His first received message since arrival. While physical contact was not going to happen, Conrad allowed for various forms of cyber contact. After purchasing

Hank's Heaven, he rented several plots of land to cellular companies, who paid him monthly for the privilege. Each was placed near the main highway before the gates, and each company was warned never to send anyone past those gates. The money generated would pay for his necessities: provisions, cellphone, and satellite tv. In other words, Conrad Nevitt shut out the world from him, but did not shut himself out from the world. Everything was on his terms.

"Are you settled?"

Jeff, the only person he actually liked anymore, simple and to the point. The great thing about Jeff was he wouldn't dare use "R U" in his text – they shared a detest for the bastardization of the English language that went back to both having grammar drill sergeants for parents. They shared many similarities, and when Conrad apprised Jeff of his plan to drop out of society, Jeff's comment was simply, "I'm jealous." Conrad knew that to be true, and knew his friend would love to have done this himself, but family and societal responsibilities prevented it. Given the same circumstances, Conrad wouldn't have been able to either, and their mutual understanding of each other's circumstances bonded them further.

Jeff might be the one person who could come on the property and Conrad wouldn't shoot...might be.

Jeff would understand either way.

"I am fine."

Chapter 4...First Day (The Big Lake)

The couch in front of the fireplace invited naptime. Conrad always enjoyed the family tradition of power napping, and seemed healthier during those times when a thirty-to-ninety minute afternoon nap took place. Now, plenty of time to get naps into the schedule.

Lying down, thoughts embraced the relaxation. For one of the few times in life, no hurry...to do anything. Daydreaming, once a part-time fixture to maintain a hold on sanity, now became a fixture. Anytime people deemed necessary, dream about them and then let them go away as quickly as they entered.

Conrad looked at his phone: 2:10. Eyes closed.

Conrad looked at his phone: 3:05. Nap over.

Did he want food? Happy Hour? Fishing? More daydreaming? Whatever, he realized one goal achieved: do whatever floated the boat. With that, he wondered if the canoe floated. Hauled by trailer through several states, he wondered if any damage was done. Now another question: which of the three ponds did he want to put the canoe on today? And which pond constituted the permanent site?

Decisions, decisions, and then realization no decision was the proper course. Nada. Do whatever he damned well pleased whenever he damned well pleased. Conrad realized acquiescing to this lifestyle took time – the frantic pace set for decades no longer ruled. Hell, he didn't have to end naptime, and sleep didn't have to be at night. Bedtime could be, say, 11:00 a.m. and lunch could be, say, 2:30 a.m.

The rules flew out the window, up the chimney, whatever metaphor came to mind. Conrad owned his own time and basked in that thought. Still, he desired to get up and felt no animosity toward the normal societal timeline, so at this point, the societal timeline would be kept. Rising, he glanced out the window. No animals dining yet. He knew it would take time as they would need to overcome the fear he appeared to already put aside. A little fear, however, remained a good thing and he needed to realize he was in their universe – not the other way around. That might change as time progressed but, at this time, the universe was theirs.

The rods and reels remained in the canoe, and, since he hadn't ventured to the third lake, it was probably time. He loved the dirt road, remembering Jeff Foxworthy's "You might be a redneck if directions to your house include get off the paved road." He wondered how long before the road would be in disrepair. He knew little about road repair but knew he wouldn't have anyone out to work on it – that would violate his personal vow. Conrad would simply cross that bridge (literally and figuratively) when coming to it. Fortunately, no bridges needed for the three-quarters-of-a-mile trek to the "Big Lake", as the family called it due to its stature among the three ponds.

The Big Lake (which he thought needed a better name) was at least three times larger than either of the other ponds, and logically held the biggest fish. Conrad's first-ever fish was caught in this lake, as his three year-old self pulled a bluegill out of the waters, using a cane pole and a worm. That fish made it all the way home. For some reason, his parents let him take it home. They had to know it couldn't survive in his makeshift tin can of lake water, but he guessed they indulged him and threw the fish away after he went to bed that night. He didn't remember details, but sufficed that they told him a believable story about the fish – not hard to fool a three year-old.

As he drove up onto the dam of The Big Lake (which needed a better name), he viewed the spot where the first fish was caught. The lake was a bit different from his childhood, the Army Corps of Engineers building up the dam two decades ago. They widened an interstate highway nearby and had no place to put the dirt. Uncle Hank, a longtime Corps employee, talked them into using the dirt to build up the dam. They complied, and the result was more beauty than ever. Walden could have his pond, Conrad believed this to be the prettiest place on earth. Unspoiled except for one two-person bench on the bank opposite the dam, The Big Lake brought Conrad to tears.

I own this...I really own this...Uncle Hank, I will protect it always.

Realtors came out of the woodwork when Hank died, as they schemed to turn 250 acres into 150 homes. One more rape of the land and Conrad couldn't take one more rape of the land. Everything fell into place for the purchase and the timing seemed God-given.

This place will never be spoiled by humanity.

Driving to the end of the dam, he backed the trailer to water's edge. The canoe straps undone, the watercraft slid easily into the water in a place Conrad remembered well. He'd caught his first catfish there while his Aunt Josie, who was supposed to be watching the eight year-old, was busy trying to seduce the person who would become his Uncle Karl. It was his first time witnessing such a sight and he now understood why they remained oblivious to him catching catfish after catfish. Ironically, no catfish had been caught in the lake for years – all

25

bass, crappie, and bluegill. Conrad believed catfish were still there, but the people allowed to fish there, and they were few in numbers, were all bass fishermen, so no one had actually tried for catfish. He hoped some of the originals, especially those he released, remained.

Conrad used three rods when fishing. One always had an artificial nightcrawler, one always had a topwater lure, and one always had some type of "real" bait. In this case, nightcrawlers graced the hook and he would troll the live bait behind the canoe while casting one of the artificial-laden lines into his favorite bass spots. Softly, Conrad put the paddle into the water and began the trip around the Big Lake. He stopped paddling to drift near one of his favorite spots, where felled trees gave rise to some of the biggest freshwater fish he'd caught.

The topwater rapala (his favorite lure) plunked in front of a not-quite-submerged log a few feet from shore. He twitched the line slightly and, to no surprise, saw the familiar whirlpool splash of a hungry bass fooled. Immediately he set the hook and, after a couple of athletic leaps, the bass went deep. A few minutes later, Conrad lifted the bass into the boat and thanked him for being so cooperative.

"Mr. Bass, I own this land, but you and your brothers continue to own this lake. I will only take one of your brothers when I am hungry and need food. Otherwise, you are free to do as you will. This is your lucky day, or as lucky as it can be with a treble hook in your mouth, because I am not hungry and simply wanted the thrill of the catch."

With that, Conrad lifted the bass to his face, bid the creature goodbye, and gently placed it back in the water. The fish made a bit of a splash, lightly dousing the fisherman.

"Can't blame you for that. If someone stuck a hook in me, I'd try to do worse, I'm sure. Thanks for the competition."

Two trips around the lake netted several bass and a couple of bluegill – all on the topwater lure. Conrad's hunger called and he readied for the end of the expedition when a creature of the deep zinged the drag on the live bait rod. A big jerk on the rod produced…

…a line without a hook. Whatever the creature was, it remained swimming. Nearly turning the canoe over with the fierceness of his yank, Conrad paused for a moment, his body a mixture of adrenaline and respect. Whatever the creature was, it was huge. Conrad remembered Uncle Hank's stories about some big carp placed in the lake over two decades ago to help with keeping the algae in line. From time to time, big fish wallowed near the surface in the middle, but Conrad had never actually seen one of them. They would definitely eat a nightcrawler.

It was his guess one just did. Conrad realized there would come another time. Thinking in other terms, he hypothesized the creature might have been a huge catfish lurking in the depths – not a carp at all, but one of the ancient fish a small boy once released unharmed back into the lake.

The decision to leave the canoe at The Big Lake made, Conrad unhooked the trailer, making sure to oil and cover the trailer before leaving. He wanted these things here for a long time, and minor care now kept from major care later. Not always known for taking care of things, Conrad now felt different – these were his things and he never wanted them replaced. This was his land, his lake, his time…A great first day.

Chapter 5...First Night

Absurd as it sounded, Conrad Nevitt decided on a romantic dinner for his first night as owner of Hank's Heaven – romantic for himself. Intimacy takes many forms, and the pure love he enjoyed for this place needed celebration. Candlelight dinner, soft music, and serenity provide a solid combination for any such occasion.

This night would never come again – first night.

Everyone seemed to be into propane and propane accessories these days, or utilizing the convenience of a George Foreman grill, but those weren't Conrad's preferences; granted, he owned two GF grills and used them quite often for quick cooking, but when it came to special occasions, nothing beat old fashion charcoal briquettes in a cheap grill. Lighter fluid, old newspapers, and aluminum foil took him back to the 1960s family barbecues. Once a week, the family gathered for burgers, hot dogs, and/or pork chops and/or steaks (depending upon the week's budget) cooked over the hot coals. In the 90s, Conrad re-instigated the tradition, hosting the family two or three times a month – always briquettes. Only once a problem – a rainy day with all the family inside, he erred in trying to grill under the deck of the back porch. Worrying about the rain getting into the grill, he doused the briquettes with a bit too much lighter fluid, and flames shot up to the roof. Fortunately, no real damage and the event ensued without incident.

Tonight, New York strips, baked potatoes, and corn on the cob constituted the fare, and Conrad performed his ritual to perfection, using just the right blend of his special ingredients: Worcheshire sauce and Sonny's Barbecue Sauce along with Nature's Seasoning. Simple spices for a simple meal for a simple life. His other trade secret was using a fork to attack the meat while seasoning prior to the grill. Pent-up anger came out as daydreams about evil people in his life who deserved to die came into focus. In the past, he always chuckled at this vengeful side of himself, knowing he would never act upon those feelings. Somehow, he no longer believed himself incapable of physical violence on other humans. As he stuck the fork into the strip time and time again, three names dominated his anger.

He believed himself capable of killing any of the three.

Two of the three were con artists who succeeded in defrauding him out of money and time. The third was simply evil incarnate under the guise of a good Samaritan – the phoniest of all. He imagined their deaths…slow and knowing their murderer – no, their executioner – and knowing why they deserved their fates. As Schwarzenneger said, "Dey were all bad."

The music selection varied, as his recent Wal-Mart spree included a revolving CD player. The five-disc player contained his five favorite artists: Jimmy Buffett, Jim Croce, The Eagles, John Denver, and David Abrams. Buffett and Croce moved him out of depression time and time again over the years – always positive memories whenever their voices rang through his ears. The Eagles, especially with Joe Walsh's guitar on "Hotel California", gave him a peaceful, easy feeling (pun intended). Denver's "Poems, Prayers, and Promises" was one of his favorite all-time songs, and "Annie's Song" and "Sunshine on My Shoulders" seldom failed to bring tears in memory of a particular lady at two particular times in his life. David Abrams was a former student and the most talented human he'd encountered. Abrams never sought the limelight, and thus never achieved it, but his talent was on par with any of these. Conrad's music collection ran the gamut of performers from Alice Cooper to Z Z Top (pun intended again), with the Beatles, Linda Ronstadt, Harry Chapin and Chicago in between (but obviously not in that alphabetical order). Pop, country, classical, jazz, indie, grunge, rap, it didn't matter as long as it fit whatever mood maintained at the time. Elvis, Sinatra, B.B. King, Ella Fitzgerald and Carly Simon filled voids at time. Conrad did a mean Louis Armstrong imitation, although often he thought people were laughing more at him than with him. Diamond, Streisand (he was not gay), Manilow (well, maybe gayer than once thought), and the Zach Brown Band also found their way into his eclectic collection. Tonight was a special night all-around, so his Fab Five were on.

Food cooked, music playing, and candles lit, Conrad placed his plate on the tv tray in front of the tv hung on a particular wall for best viewing while eating. Since college, tv trays, food and tv encompassed guilty pleasures and these were things for which he never apologized. Sitcoms, documentaries, history channels, and sports events would keep him in touch with the real world (if there was such a thing) entertainment-wise, while his laptop and Ipad would give him his daily doses (fixes) of news. Tonight he would watch his beloved Tampa Bay HooRays while listening to the music (although Dwayne Staats, Brian Anderson, and Todd Kalas were three of the few announcers to whom he actually enjoyed listening). Sometimes the sound needed to be off and the music needed to be played.

Tonight was such a night.

The meal finished just before Buffett's *He Went to Paris* played, so Conrad postponed dishwashing until the song finished. For a moment, he kicked back on the couch and enjoyed his favorite all-time song. After all these years, new meaning came at the end of the song with the lyrics "Now he lives in the islands, fishes the pylons, and drinks his green label each day...writing his memoirs, losing his hearing, but he don't care what most people say. 'Cause through 86 years of perpetual motion, he'll laugh and he'll smile and he'll say, Jimmy, some of it's magic, some of it's tragic, but I've had a good life all the way."

Dishes washed, HooRays a 2-1 winner, and the music still playing, Conrad debated couch vs. bed – a debate years running. At one point in his life, the couch normally won, but these days the bed seemed to claim the upper-hand. Besides, his first night owning Hank's Heaven meant doing everything the right way – his way.

With everything turned off, noises remained dominant, except that instead of sounds from his favorite musicians, Conrad heard his other favorite sounds: crickets, an occasional owl, bullfrogs on the water, a few small splashing noises, and a slight breeze gently maneuvering through the pines. The old air conditioning unit, as opposed to the new one installed in the A-frame, sang a song too much like his least favorite artists. Plus, he didn't trust the old unit not to burst into flames in the middle of the night, possibly killing him on what turned out to be a day that lived up to his own hype. Despite the temp being a bit more than he was used to, Conrad crawled underneath a light blanket. Since childhood, a blanket was always necessary for him to sleep soundly regardless of temperature. He looked a few feet across the room as the blinds allowed a simply ray of moonlight through. Pondering getting up and looking out the window that overlooked the pond, Conrad realized how comfortable the bed was, so he denied himself what he figured would have been a marvelous view of the moonlight on the small pond (the small pond needed a name). He scrunched the pillow as

31

always, and as usual, tried to sleep on his left side, but eventually turned to his right. For some reason, he could only sleep on his right side.

Just as the turn was made, a low growl invaded the air outside. Never great on judging distance in sound, Conrad couldn't discern whether or not the growl came from near or far. A second growl met his ears, then moments later, a third – all coming from the same place and the same creature.

Conrad arose and moved to the window. Opening the blinds, Conrad Nevitt didn't know at first whether to shriek in terror or smile in satisfaction. Indeed, the moonlight shining down on the small pond (the small pond needed a name) painted the masterpiece envisioned, but he wasn't prepared for the addendum to the painting.

On its haunches facing the water sat the big cat. He appeared master over this nightly domain. Conrad wondered if this nightly ritual would cease once the big cat realized someone was living in the cabin. He wondered if he should speak, tap on the window, or blare the music (maybe heavy metal) to scare the feline away. Shooting the creature never entered his mind; after all, the cat was not a human and certainly not trespassing. He decided to simply let the creature be. Movement to close the blinds caused the animal to turn. Another low growl, but not an angry one.

The big cat seemed to acknowledge Conrad's presence and moved to a place parallel to and exactly halfway between the cabin and the pond.

The animal laid down and went to sleep.

Conrad watched over the animal for a few minutes, mystified by its mere presence and mesmerized by its sheer beauty. Measuring at least seven feet, with paws that would make Johnny Bench do a double-take, he (or maybe she, Conrad wasn't versed in animal gender) portrayed the picture of calm and serenity. For a moment, the thought entered that the cat was staking out territory and might keep Conrad prisoner, but that thought was fleeting and pushed aside as lunacy. This animal obviously belonged here just as much as Conrad – perhaps the animal's intuition knew the same.

The first night completed...

Chapter 6...Signs, Signs, Everywhere are Signs

In the excitement over moving into the cabin, Conrad neglected to remember one significant fact. When a sixty year-old man hears the call of nature at three in the morning, he prefers the convenience of indoor plumbing. Suddenly, the A-frame looked like the better choice, regardless of the omens and beautiful view the cabin afforded. Plus, indoor plumbing allows one not to deal with creatures of the night.

Looking out the window, Conrad viewed the big cat sleeping – hopefully soundly. At least, he could sneak out the back door to venture toward the outhouse a short distance away. Of course, he figured the cat did not sleep soundly and could get curious about the noise of the back door and the movement toward the outhouse. The last thing he wanted was to shoot the animal, but survival instinct necessitated at least taking the gun.

I can do this...hell, I used to sneak in the wee hours of the morning past a sleeping detective and his wife. Thought I was stealth as a native American for quite some time during my teen years, until that breakfast conversation right after Mom left the table.

"Boy, you're keeping awfully late hours."

"I know, sir, but I'm very quiet coming in."

"Not quiet enough for me, boy. Here's the deal: I don't care what time you come in, but if your Mom wakes and complains, your ass is mine. As long as she never says anything, it's your life."

"Thank you, sir."

"But, anybody out after midnight is looking for trouble."

"I understand."

"Make sure you do. Of course, I'm not amused you're drinking at your age."

"What makes you think that?"

"Well, boy, I'm smelling 100 proof Knob Creek after you walk through the living room. Glad you're not drinking heavy – what, two or three shots?"

"Uh, yeah..."

Conrad remembered the smile streaming across his Dad's face at the satisfaction in nailing his youngest son to the wall. He also realized his fear of Dad still surpassed his fear of anything or anyone else – including the sleeping feline outside the window.

Calling upon his teen stealth abilities, Conrad made his way safely to and from the outhouse. Re-entering the bedroom, his glance out the window showed the big cat in the same place. If it moved, it hid movement well.

Two shots of Knob Creek later, the body returned to bed for a couple more hours of sleep. He wondered if he would wake at 6:15 a.m., as he had for twenty years.

Yes.

This time, the glance fell on an empty patch of ground halfway between the cabin and the small pond (the small pond needs a name). Perusing the grounds produced no sign of the big cat, and Conrad wondered if the scene would repeat itself that night. Perhaps he needed to get a small port-a-potty for the cabin.

Normally not a big breakfast person, an exception was made this day for bacon and eggs, especially since both were perishables. They were tasty and he, like his ancestors, kept the bacon grease for future cooking – a tin can provided the perfect container. Stepping out the front door, he inhaled the crispness of the air among the pine trees, letting the oxygen fill lungs too long citified. Looking around, he felt a pang of disappointment that the feeding bins remained untouched. He thought sure something would feed overnight, but then thoughts turned to the "guardian" creature at the side of the cabin.

Hmm…wonder why no animals would come when the biggest predator in the forest is right there? Doh!

Time to establish a routine. He adored routine and craved establishing a positive one in Hank's Heaven. Bringing his laptop outside, he uttered a prayer that the internet provider that came with the satellite package actually worked.

It did, showing the internet connection he asked for: HuckU2ltd.

Conrad moved to the two-seater on the dam of the small pond (which really needed a better name) and read various newspapers online: *The New York Times, The Pine City Daily News, The Tampa Bay Times, The Louisville Courier-Journal and the Hartford Courant.* The reading never took long as he picked articles based on each newspaper's strengths, especially the *PCDS* because it had the public record from his hometown. That part of the paper entertained him in knowing who had been arrested for what.

After finishing the reading, Conrad pondered what to do with the rest of the day. Living with a plan for a lifetime and now not having one proved a bit unnerving; hence, he wanted routine but wanted it to be HIS routine...positive and productive.

Or not. Lazy was an option – maybe he'd try that a while. But first, the signs.

The rest of the morning was spent hanging signs throughout the property. He bought a variety, as was his custom, but each carried the same message:

NO TRESPASSING!

Still, he couldn't resist being creative with them – the advantage of having a good friend who specialized in signage. The two of them dreamed up a plethora of messages. Signs were placed next to the standard NO TRESPASSING:

- No Trespassing (DOUBLE WARNING)

- Beware of Owner

- Beware of Owner with a Gun

- Keep Out! This means you – I have no friends anymore

- Anyone on this property not named Conrad Nevitt will be shot

- Before entering this property, make sure your next of kin knows where you are

- Open Season on Trespassers

- Looking for Heads to Mount on My Wall

- Owner hoping to play Hannibal Lector in the sequel

- State Statute says if you're standing here, I can kill you

- Trespasser Burial Ground

With each sign, the "Signs" song rang through his head. "Signs, signs, everywhere are signs...blockin' out the scenery..."

He hoped the final hang would eliminate the song and eliminate trespassers. The last thing Conrad wanted was company and he determined to make anyone with nerve enough to enter his property: DEAD. None of his friends took him seriously when apprised – not even when he sent out a listserv e-mail quoting the state statute giving owners of property in this area the right to "stand their ground".

As Conrad Nevitt strolled back to the cabin, singing "Do this, don't do that...can't you read the signs?", he wondered who the first idiot would be.

Chapter 7...Firing the First Shot

Positive routine came easily over the next 12 days. Conrad established virtually everything wanted in a day, and relished that no human interfered. Whether or not animals interfered never worried him, feeling these creatures established their routines long before he invaded their territory. He remembered Hank telling stories of animals who came and went randomly, often simply walking up to the A-frame door seemingly to say hello or to see if Hank was there. The oddity of the story rested in Hank's insistence that no animal ever sped away scared.

They understood Hank – Hank understood them.

The daily routine was established:

- 6:15   wakeup
- 6:30   morning constitutional
- 6:30-7:00   breakfast
- 7:00-7:30   a walk around the grounds
- 7:30-9:30   online reading
- 9:30-12:30   fishing one pond or the others (they really needed names)
- 12:30-1:15   lunch
- 1:15-2:00 or 2:15 or 2:30 or 2:45 or 3:00   nap
- 3:00-5:00   chores (whatever needed to be done that day)
- 5:00-7:00   writing
- 7:00-7:30   dinner

- 7:30-10:30   television

- 10:30   bed

Like clockwork, every night when Conrad went to bed, the low growl emanated outside, and he would tap the window to acknowledge the big cat's presence. The big cat would turn and take his place upon the throne known as the area halfway between the cabin and the small pond (the small pond truly needed a name). A port-a-potty placed in the kitchen eliminated the middle-of-the-night problem, and emptying it every morning became part of the routine. The big cat always left before 6:15, and Conrad asked no questions – no greater comfort against looters than having a big cat looming every night, and Conrad knew no fear of the animal.

He probably calls me Hank Jr.

At that thought, bad humor set in.

All my rowdy friends haven't settled down – I've eliminated them from my life.

While a bit surprised no one called his bluff yet and checked on him, his message rang loud and clear he was not to be bothered and the consequences for bothering him would be dire. Still, people in general never seem to believe rules apply to them as individuals no matter who sets the rules. Everyone thinks they're the exception.

He wondered who the first exception would be – he possessed no doubt of his actions when the time arose. The betting line rested with Greg, whose arrogance matched his ineptness – a horrible combination found too often in the human race. Greg, perhaps more than any of Conrad's "friends", epitomized why he left humanity behind. That "it's all about me because I'm wonderful and everyone should love me" attitude drove Conrad beyond his limits of sanity. Greg didn't think he was smarter than everyone else – he KNEW it. The Ph.D. exemplified his proof, but exemplified to Conrad that "Piled Higher and Deeper" was the correct explanation.

B.S., M.S. Ph.D.: Bullshit, Moreshit, Piled Higher and Deeper. Academicians and people with degrees think they are so superior to everyone else. I didn't become one bit better at my teaching job because I knew Charles Dickens had an affair with a cousin, or Ben Jonson was a pervert, or Lewis Carroll was a drug addict, or Hunter Thompson – well, hell, everyone knew who The Good Doctor was, and he wouldn't care anymore than I do what they thought. Read the writing – it's not about the writer – it's the writing.

The one element of humanity he thought he might miss was teaching. The classroom constituted the one place where he'd seen the best in people. His irritation with humanity grew from his generation bad-mouthing students. In a class of 30, 20-25 worked hard. That's a damned good percentage and higher than the regular populace of any 30 people. Why did these people teach if they hated students? He left the profession before he hated students. People he hated, not students. He understood the paradox. Students as students weren't real people because they were conveying their good sides only in order to get ahead. Unfortunately, the world would soon corrupt them and they would become real people.

Then Conrad could hate them.

The clock read 1:15, lunch consumed (two nutritious peanut butter and jelly sandwiches with a Pepsi), and time for a nap. Conrad looked out the front window and saw several animals dining at the various bins. As expected, it took a while for them to feel comfortable with him there, but the menagerie began establishing a couple of days prior. Today's group included a couple of raccoons, a doe, some turkey, and the ever-present birds. He shook his head at himself for thinking one of the birds, a blue heron, was a friend of his from Florida. The Florida heron, whom he nicknamed Scotty because it reminded him of a person in his life that always looked for something for nothing, flew the same erratic takeoff as this particular bird. Scotty's markings included a scar under his left wing – obviously from a non-eco-friendly fisherman too lazy to collect his own discarded line. So many birds injured simply because humans don't care. Conrad hadn't gotten close enough to this bird to ascertain whether or not the scar was in the same place. He liked thinking it was Scotty so didn't want proof it wasn't.

As he turned to head into the bedroom for the daily nap, a purple light blinked into his eyes – the light he figured would light sooner than it had. The light signified a large creature entered the periphery of Hank's Heaven. The sensors set at various locations only went off when something over 100 pounds entered.

Looks like my engineering classes finally paid dividends.

Without hesitation, Conrad picked up his weapon and headed out the door. Naptime delayed, the time came to make good on his promise to himself and everyone else. The monitor next to the purple blinking light read "Main Gate", so he knew confrontation would now begin. Opening the door, he viewed a tall drink of water still fumbling at getting all the way over the second gate. He wondered how problematic the first gate, the one that set off the purple light, was for his non-athletic former friend.

Conrad heard the intruder curse and curse some more. Conrad hoped the intruder would say something else out loud, not relishing in the fact that the man's last words would include taking God's name in vain. Perhaps confrontation and allowing the man to say something else would be appropriate; after all, this was the first test of Conrad's resolve, and no rulebook existed for how to achieve the end goal.

Gun focused on its target, movement continued as the two men closed distance. Greg Maharis spotted his friend and the gun.

"Don't shoot! It's only me!"

"You never were good at following directions, were you, Greg?"

"Not my strong suit. Besides, I never believed you capable of killing anyone. You're not MacBeth or any other Shakespearean murderer."

"No, but wouldn't you say I've always been a man of my word?"

"Well, yes, that's a truity."

The two men stood a few paces from each other, gun still pointed.

"Are you going to put the gun down?

"If you hadn't taken the Lord's name in vain, I would have already shot you – didn't want those words to be your last."

"Oh, c'mon, Conrad, I'm your best friend. You're not going to shoot your best friend. Let's have some Knob Creek and talk about old times."

"Greg, you are and always have been an arrogant prick. If you don't think you are, let me give you the proof: you're standing as a trespasser on my land when I told you in writing NO ONE was to visit and told you in writing NO ONE coming on to my land would escape without dire consequences. Only your arrogance would make you believe I'm not going to shoot you."

Conrad, for the first time, felt Greg becoming realistic about the situation.

"Conrad, be civilized."

"In a civilized society, people would adhere to the rules set by the person who owns the land. I own the land, and you should have adhered to my rules. Therefore, I am being civilized. But there is one thing I want you to do."

"Anything."

"I want you to be Marlon Brando for a moment...I want you to act out one word from *Streetcar*...I want you to yell 'Stella' at the top of your lungs. Do that for me."

"STELLA! STELLA! ST—"

The shot rang true.

Chapter 8...Guilty of Being True to One's Word

Conrad prepared in advance for the trial he knew forthcoming. He knew before the shot that the state would put him on trial for at least the first shooting. This first trial would set a precedent and perhaps keep other trials from taking place. Confident in his stance after reading all state statutes and confident in his attorney's grasp of the issue, Conrad hoped this would be the only time arrested. Of the verdict, he possessed no doubts.

His attorney, the Honorable James David Goldstein, made a successful career out of getting the worst of humanity out of whatever charges faced. While his advertising campaigns comprised creativity and catchiness, the tv and newspaper slogans paled in comparison to his real mantra: "If you're innocent, hire Woodrow Rapier; if you're guilty, hire me."

Goldstein remained a friend through the years, possibly because he maintained so few friends. People turned off at his pomposity, brashness, and all the qualities that made him marvelous at this job. Conrad saw through the business façade at the true nature of the man: passionate about what he did and passionate about sticking it to the corruption of the legal system.

Conrad's kind of man and one of the few he still liked.

Knowing the set of events, the two researched for months prior to Conrad settling into Hank's Heaven, so they were beyond prepared when courtroom time came. Only one worry came to Conrad's mind, a quote from the great Mark Twain: "We have a criminal jury system which is superior to any in the world; and its efficiency is only marred by the difficulty of finding twelve men every day who don't know anything and can't read."

Goldstein assuaged the doubts, apprising that jury selection would be no problem, as most people believed in the concept of man protecting his property, and there were a number of precedents in the county for Conrad's action. The law, legal precedent, and a jury selected by Goldstein comprise an easy non-guilty verdict.

Still, Conrad remained a bit antsy despite the confidence of before. The prosecuting attorney made a great case for pre-meditation, presenting the listserve as one of the major exhibits foreshadowing the accused's intention to commit murder.

However, when it came the defense's turn, Goldstein deftly destroyed each piece of evidence, one by one, hammering home the right of a human to decide what goes on his property, and who goes on his property. References to Libertarianism, the Founding Fathers, the Flag, the National Rifle Association, and Doctor Hunter S. Thompson wove into the defense like a finely tuned piano. James David Goldstein lived his life for a trial of this scope, and he enjoyed the time of his life presenting his case.

The only major source of debate concerned whether or not the defendant would take the stand. Conrad desired to defend himself, but Goldstein remained adamant that the case was cut and dry and could turn badly should he slip on the witness stand. They played the mock interview, and Conrad realized that the prosecution might be able to sway the jury based on the lack of remorse within Conrad. He wasn't going to perjure – he contained no remorse -- and while he considered himself a decent actor (better than Greg's "Stella" debacle), realized his attorney felt the case was won and there was no need to take chances.

Conrad Nevitt failed to take the stand.

The trial lasted only a few days, and only one night in jail spent. Anticipating the arrest, Conrad made bail/bond money available to his attorney well in advance, and even the sheriff seemed surprise at the speed of release.

Conrad possessed a myriad of faults – advanced preparation never seemed to be one of them.

The prosecution's closing argument took an inordinate amount of time and was full of tired clichés and legalese. Conrad watched the jury and became buoyed by their boredom, although he kept the face of innocence demanded by Goldstein.

"Don't let them see you proud of yourself. Act like you did something that had to be done and, while you're not happy about doing it, you feel you acted appropriately. Act a bit sad about shooting Greg even if, as we both know, you're not."

He worked on that face and felt he nailed it – he realized his hypocrisy in his acting, but justified it by telling himself he really didn't want to kill Greg, and was sorry in a sense to do it, but it had to be done.

At least, that's what he told himself and it worked for him.

When it came time for the defense's closing argument, James David Goldstein's reticence never wavered:

"Gentlemen and Gentle Ladies of the jury, this is a cut and dry trial. You must decide whether or not my client, who has lived one of the most honorable lives any of us has known, has the right after a life of service to his friends, his states, and his country, to live out his days alone on his property without interference from the outside world. That's all he wants – simply to be left alone and be allowed to live out his days in peace and quiet following sixty-two years of complete and devoted service to all of us. We all agree he has the right to defend his property and his isolation and he told everyone to leave him be – to let him rest.

Honorable members of this jury, you are entrusted today to determine whether or not a person possesses the right to live their final years as no bother to anyone – to live their final years away from society, and to be able to protect and preserve the right to live alone without fear of invasion – without fear of attack – to be able to live in peace and harmony in nature and not bother anyone unless someone tramples on that right to live in peace and harmony in nature.

Conrad Nevitt is the most honorable man any of us have ever known. His life was spent in dedication to educating young minds and serving whatever community was fortunate enough to have him as a citizen. For 62 years, he lived his life for everyone else without asking for anything in return.

Now, he comes to you, the honorable citizens of this county, and for the first time in his life, asks for something in return for all the good works he's done.

He wants us to let him live his remaining days on the place he considers heaven on earth, devoid of people and the perpetrations and over-the-top demands they place on individuals of Conrad's giving personality.

Conrad Nevitt deserves his time alone. You, the honorable members of the jury, have the opportunity to grant his one wish and fortify a law we all agree with: that a man has the right to defend his property from anyone who would invade his ground. All Conrad Nevitt

wants is to be able to stand his ground...and it is his ground...just as your ground is your ground.

Let him keep his ground. Thank you."

The verdict returned in only a few hours.

"Not guilty."

Chapter 9...Repercussions

Returning to Hank's Heaven following the acquittal, Conrad received a surprising amount of communication from people across the country. The overwhelming majority of letters, texts and facadebook posts complimented him for such things as "...exercising your God-given right to stand your ground" and "...establishing parameters and living by them" to simple "You did nothing wrong" and "I would have done the same thing and now I might do it myself."

Negative communications came as well. "Murderer", "I hope you rot in hell", and "He who lives by the gun dies by the gun" were among those taking exception to his actions, but these were far fewer than the positive comments. Several life-threatening communications came in, and those were turned over to authorities for what he speculated would be non-investigations. Local, state and federal authorities had better things to do than spend time on anonymous correspondences. No one who threatened gave any clue as to who they were but warned Conrad he would never see them coming. Unnerving as the threats left him, he knew life continued and one couldn't live one's life worried about other people; after all, people were no longer part of his existence.

The one that unnerved the most centered on a Twitter post. It wasn't the message that bothered him – it was the hashtag. The Twitter simply read, "People think they can hide behind the law or exploit the law or simply use it to their advantage. Conrad Nevitt deserves punishment". That, in itself, at least was well written in Conrad's mind, and the writer was obviously a person of intelligence. But the signature #Iwilltortureandexecuteconradnevitt caused beads of sweat, goosebumps and all other nervous "twitters" to form. This made the message worth remembering and caused him to make his first outside contact since moving to Hank's Heaven.

One of Conrad's best friends in life spent a lifetime with the Central Intelligence Agency. Now retired, John Ray Jenkins operated a private detective agency out of Chicago. John Ray remained trusted, so a call was made.

"John Ray, Conrad here."

"Mr. Newsmaker, how the hell are you?"

"Free and isolated, thank you. I need a favor."

"You? You need a favor. Thought you'd excommunicated all of us mere mortals...don't want anything to do with us."

"I don't, but you remember Mom quoted necessity is the mother of invention, and my situation necessitates your inventiveness."

"What's up?"

After apprising Jenkins of the situation, Conrad asked for the next step.

"The next step is simple: you hire me to find this character."

"How much? Name your price."

"Don't want money. Want a favor."

"Name it."

"You won't like it one bit."

"Desperate times call for desperate measures. What is the favor?"

"Hire me."

"You're hired."

"When it's over, I'll cash in the favor, but you won't like it."

"When this is over, I'll be happy to cash. I've already compromised my personal vow by making first contact with you, but then, we always screwed with the status quo, didn't we?"

"That we did – had a good time doing it."

"Not bad for a couple of guys from the Mayberry of our state."

"Not bad at all. Send me everything you have and I'll get to work on it."

"Don't you mean you'll get **your people** to work on it?"

"No, just me. The less people know about this investigation, the better, and this way I can handle this person as I see fit. Besides, I still owe you, remember?"

"Didn't plan to bring that up and you don't owe me anything."

"But you will after I find this person and dispose of them."

"Dispose?"

"We're not that different, you and me...never were. I need to get started. I'll contact you when the deal is done and you owe me."

Other than the one twitter message that now seemed in great hands, Conrad paid attention to but remained unconcerned about other social media. The internet arguments intrigued him, as Conrad diligently read them and enjoyed the high-level dialogue from both sides of the issue. Posts on Facadebook reminded him of various classroom discussions over the years on such things as capital punishment, The Ten Commandments, and individual freedoms. People from all races, creeds and areas represented their beliefs well on these timelines, and Conrad found them educational and somewhat inspirational. Of course, the timelines also contained their fair share of idiots who failed to write a complete sentence, failed to spell anything correctly, and who let emotion interfere with competency. Those were not taken seriously.

None changed his mind about whether or not he was right, because that was a moot point: in his mind, he was following his own course, so right and wrong were superfluous issues. Whether anyone agreed with his course paled in comparison with following that course.

The one aspect of the virality of the circumstances laid in becoming nationally known. The trial made all the alphabets: CNN, NBC, CBS, ABC, Fox and others. HBO messaged him about a documentary, and several networks wanted him to star in a reality series. All of this attention comprised his worst nightmare – he desired isolation, not fame. Politely responding to each, the response generated remained "No". One network made the mistake of sending a camera crew past the first gate. Two cameras setup on the second gate never will be used again, as bulletholes are hard to repair.

"Hey, what do you think you're doing?"

"Sorry cameraman, I missed...I was aiming for you. I won't miss again."

No cameras returned – contrary to his words, the aim proved true and effective.

Unfortunately, Conrad now earned the status of hero or villain, depending upon one's viewpoint. He knew himself neither and became more adamant about being alone. He considered a moratorium on the internet, but decided on the importance of keeping up-to-date on what people in the world were doing. Much easier to keep them at bay if he knew where the bay resided. Besides, he admitted to himself being continuously curious about public perception on his venture, and knew that his few days of fame would fade with the next made-up world crisis. The media method always entailed beating a story beyond death, but once a ratings point slipped a modicum, the media moved to the next story.

As the Eagles sang, "They will never forget you until somebody new comes along."

He waited with great anticipation for that somebody new to come along.

Chapter 10...A Return to Near Normalcy

Never say never. One of Conrad Nevitt's axioms was he could never be surprised by anything. Still, if someone told him that a crisis in the Middle East would benefit him personally, he would come back on his "never surprised" axiom. But such events transpired to make that happen.

A conflict arose between two Middle Eastern countries, becoming all the rage of every network and every media outlet in existence. Suddenly, Conrad was not simply old news – he was no news.

Conrad became thankful for the Middle East.

Normalcy returned. No more Facadebook discussion, no more letters, and no more tweets. For the next several weeks, he lived his life in complete and total isolation. Continuing to live in the cabin, the routine so well established in the early part of this adventure returned to fruition. His only non-internet contact with the outside world came when picking up provisions ordered from Wal-Mart and left at the base of the first gate. No delivery person ever availed themselves to be seen, probably sensing a fate similar to Greg's. The delivery truck sounded its horn three times after dropoff. Conrad wasn't quite sure whether it was the signal the provisions were delivered or relief from the driver for getting the hell out of Dodge.

As with many things these days, Conrad failed to care.

His care centered on the menagerie formed around both structures. The animals gravitated more to the A-frame than the cabin, but he surmised a simple physical answer: the scent from the big cat hung around the cabin, and any animal in its right mind would avoid that predator at all costs. Conrad didn't understand why he wasn't more fearful – the cat represented a superior predator capable of mincing him into at least a couple of meals. But the two seemed to bond over the nightly growl, tap on the window and sleep side by side regimen. Of course, Conrad valued the structure providing the barrier between them at night.

Funny thing: his monthly grocery bill showed more spent on animal food than human food; of course, not only did they outnumber, they all seemed to enjoy dining...and he enjoyed feeding them. He realized the irony in substituting serving the animal kingdom rather than serving humanity but another Twainism came to mind: "If you take a dog in and make him prosperous, he will not bite you – that is the principle difference between a dog and a man." Conrad also smiled at the irony that of all the animals who regularly dined in his yard, none were dogs. Still, an apt aphorism.

The good news centered on the progress made in their comfortability with him. He strolled freely through the yard surrounding the A-frame, filling the bins of food for the various members of what was becoming a tribe. A lounge chair purchased, placed strategically in the midst of the feeding areas, never stopped the buffet – never slowed the eating. The only surprising members of the menagerie were the armadillos, who weren't native creatures to this region.

Guess nobody bothered to tell them, and they either didn't read the manual, or disregarded the instructions on where to live.

The blue heron, Scotty, apparently flew south as the weather began to change. Conrad wished he could have been this close to the bird as he was to these animals, for then he could inspect that wing and verify it was his bird. Perhaps the spring would see Scotty's return.

The animals also appeared to like his music – especially Buffett's sound. Strange as it was to Conrad, and perhaps it was simply coincidence, but every time "Come Monday" played, animals came into view – especially the deer. By the time the song was halfway through, several deer would be in relaxation position in the yard. So Conrad always played it through at least twice before the rest of the CD played.

Perhaps he gave off a better vibe when Buffett music played. Animals certainly pick up on those things better than humans.

Hell, animals are better than humans.

Conrad looked forward to his first fall at Hank's Heaven – looked forward to the full colorful foliage of the forest primeval surrounding him. Some of the trees showed a head start even though fall's start was still a bit away. Memories of marvelous fall days here during his childhood flooded back...along with one of horror he never eradicated but seemed to have a mental block about. A college instructor taught him about repressed memories – this one stayed repressed all these decades but now was flooding back and Conrad didn't know why.

Conrad was 10 at a time when 10 year-olds weren't watched as closely as they are today. In that time period, children left the house in the morning, came home for lunch, then went to parks, ballfields, and creeks until the streetlights summoned them home (or Moms using the full names of whoever wasn't home at dusk).

On this fall day, he and his grandmother were fishing the small pond (the small pond truly needs a name), and were catching lots of small bluegill, but nothing larger. He asked permission to walk to The Big Lake (that name might stick) that was instantly granted. Amazing how much longer a walk it was for a ten year-old than a sixty-two year-old – must have shrunk in distance over 52 years. After what seemed like forever, young Conrad looked over The Big Lake for the first time alone.

He relished the feeling. For the first of many times in his life, he felt one with nature...realizing he needed to be alone to truly feel that oneness.

Conrad remembered the energy radiating through his body that day, and then remembered the sight never to be forgotten...but for 52 years, laid dormant in the recesses of the one true personal computer.

It happened as he moved across the dam, a much smaller dam than today's. Surveying the lake for the best place to cast the bait on the end of the line attached to his Zebco 202, he spotted something gray sticking out of the water – a new tree must have fallen into the water, providing structure for big bass.

He moved closer to the gray object and, with each step, a stench became more prevalent in his nostrils. Realization that the large object was a dead animal hit home. Conrad quickened his pace, and tripped on a log, falling partially into the water and catching his foot in the muck. Now a few feet away, he saw the convoy of flies gathered on the carcass and then achieved what every 10 year-old would achieve given this set of circumstances.

Gagging followed by vomiting dropped him to his knees, bent over and clutching his stomach. Finally gathering himself, he grabbed his Zebco and raced back across the dam and along the ditch-laden road back to the small pond.

As he worked to overcome his sickness, he heard a loud moan coming from the hillside. He didn't know whether to explore or not. It simply sounded like a kitten whining for its mother. With the scene before him, no chances needed to be taken.

"Grandaddy! Grandmother! Uncle Hank! Come quick. Something's dead in the big lake!"

He nearly hyperventilated as the trio tried to calm the boy, finally settling him down with a drink of Falstaff Beer. Conrad remembered how nasty that beer was – but it must have been on sale at Kroger's that week.

Conrad remembered not wanting to go back, but they didn't want to leave him alone in his mental state, and they were all going to see what it was. Uncle Hank drove his pickup truck like a madman – even driving up on the dam, which no one did in those days, and speeding over to the edge. Young Conrad and his grandmother remained in the truck while the two older men inspected the site.

Amazement was the young boy's emotion as he stared at Uncle Hank walking into the water and simply dragging the fly-infested, stench-laden, rotting animal to the shore. However, his grandfather's words caught more attention.

"Dammit to hell, Hank, there's a damned body in the water."

To each person's surprise and horror, a body floated to the surface, and Conrad saw Hank's face sink in realization of whom it was. His grandfather immediately placed his large hand on Hank's shoulder.

"Damn, Hank."

The two exchanged sad, knowing glances, and together retrieved the body from the water.

It was the one and only time, until his own arrest by the state police, that Conrad saw police authorities on Hank's Heaven. Emergency vehicles of all types were present with lights flashing and medical teams and cops and all kinds of questions.

Hours later, his grandparents escorted him into his parents' house, where his grandfather told them all he knew. Conrad could remember the last part of his grandfather's story.

"...damnedest site I ever saw, and I've seen a man decapitated on railroad tracks. When Hank pulled the animal out of the water, the body came up to the surface. The cops say from what they first saw that he must have fought the animal – he got a knife into it that killed it but they were probably already in the water and when the big animal fell, it knocked the man cold. The weird part is they didn't find any scratch marks on him and that both had gunshot wounds. No gun was found and the cops thought it might have just drifted out to the middle of the lake. They tried finding it but didn't get anything off the bottom but stumps. Both had been there a few days before Con found them stinkin' to high heaven – nasty shit."

Young Conrad repressed the memory for years, but now realized why he so vividly remembered now.

The animal was a big cat...the man's name was Peter Payne, named after the frontier ancestor. He was Uncle Hank's first cousin and often roamed the hills, and often without Hank knowing he was there. Most people said he was "different", whatever that meant, but in the world at that time it probably meant he possessed some kind of mental handicap the family kept within the family. Conrad remembered meeting Peter a couple of times and how he seemed a nice enough person, but had an air about him that made the young boy uncomfortable. He always talked about his friend, Soft Kitty, and Conrad always thought he was talking about a small kitten.

As his memories cleared, he no longer believed Soft Kitty was small. In his adult mind, he realized the gunshot wounds weren't made by Peter. Someone killed them.

Conrad looked up the hillside, and now believed some leaves turned while he was in memoryland. Everything seemed so peaceful and calm. He hoped for continued quiet time until fall and beyond.

The wish was not to be.

Chapter 11...Hamlet Redux

The portable monitor on the metal tray next to the lounge chair began blinking. This time, the gold light flickered on and off, apprising Conrad that someone was entering the property at a point nearest the interstate highway. Grabbing his gun, Conrad set off to the northwest portion of Hank's Heaven.

With each step, he pondered the next move. Would he be arrested and prosecuted again? Would he and Goldstein convince another jury this course was legal? Would he even allow police on his property again?

The one thing never entering his mind was doubt about what was going to happen next. Whoever entered took their own life by coming onto the property. Conrad mused the point of entry was especially stupid, given the sign "Anyone on this property not named Conrad Nevitt will be shot." He also mused that should the person be like his late cousin Peter, unable to read, perhaps a pass could be given.

No exceptions.

Assuming the perpetrator would journey toward the cabin or the A-frame, Conrad used the camouflaged stand between the two structures. Built in the 80s during the only time Uncle Hank allowed deer hunting on his property, the stand continued in surprisingly good condition despite Conrad's efforts to reinforce it. The planks he put down left much to be desired – he might have master carpenters in his family tree, but Conrad was not one of them.

Any manual labor I do is purely by mistake.

The Buffett lyric from *It's My Job* rang true with him, but he found himself performing more and more manual labor tasks on Hank's Heaven – and actually enjoying them. Improvement was slow in coming, but he noticed improvement each time he picked up a hammer and nails, screwdriver and screws, and anytime wood was involved. With deer season approaching, he wanted a high place from which to observe the majestic animals – no thought of shooting them ever entered his mind. This stand was only for observation, but today, returned to its roots as a place from which to spot a different type of game: AN IT (Illegal Tresspasser).

Department of Redundancy Department rears its ugly head again, but funny nonetheless.

Minutes passed before the IT came into view. Conrad sighed.

Jonathan Campbell supervised Conrad's literature department the last decade of Conrad's career. Campbell laughed when the retirement announcement came, and went so far as telling the audience at the banquet, "Conrad will never retire. He loves people too much, loves the thrill of education too much, loves what he does too much to ever get too far away from it. We'll be seeing him every semester as an adjunct, I'm sure."

One facet of academia held true over the years: the higher up an academician rose on the totem pole, the more they forgot what it was like to be in the classroom...the more they forgot what academics were all about. Supervisors, the longer time out of the classroom, the greater the disconnect with the people actually doing the academic tasks. Conrad tried supervising, and received rave reviews, but hated the job as passionately as he loved the classroom. Jonathan truly performed as one of the finest teachers around, and Conrad felt

qualified, as he had sat in Jonathan's classroom on a number of occasions. The irony that most

academic decisions made in the country were made by people who hadn't been in the

classroom since they were college students never failed to amuse and mortify him. Even within

an institution itself, seldom do the major players possess a great deal of teaching experience –

yet all portray themselves as academic experts.

Let them deal with lesbian stalkers plagiarizing from heterosexual white supremacists.

No, they want to wash those things under the bridge and act like those problems don't exist. Let

them deal with a gunman coming into the classroom that only has one exit. Oh, wait, let's have

role playing at our next overly-funded mandatory all-college workshops. That will fix the

problem of working with students who haven't bathed, eaten, or slept in days.

Conrad loved students – hated people...and when students became people, he quit

liking them.

When Jonathan moved within a few yards of the stand, Conrad decided confrontation

time was anon. He shook his head at his inner monologue becoming more Shakespearean, as

Jonathan remained the finest Shakespearean scholar Conrad knew. No regrets forthcoming

that Campbell's life would end in tragedy.

"Hark! I hear the tramplings of a scholar."

"Hi, Con, quite a place you have here. I hope you don't mind me ignoring your warning

signs – I've got a proposition for you."

"Methinks I shalt hear it to amuse myself."

"Will you come down and talk?"

"Forsooth! I shall depart mine balcony and hence parlay a face-to-face dialogue. I grow tired of the folly of my monologue and will engage thee in mirthful conversation ere you deem me a droning clapper-clawed clotpole."

"Ah, I see you've been keeping up with your Shakespearean insults."

"All the world's a stage, and we are merely players in what can be a comedy, a tragedy, or a melodrama – or any combination thereof."

As Conrad descended the stand, he sensed a growing nervousness in Campbell. Perhaps the knowledge of what happened to Greg coupled with the view of the same gun used caused the uneasiness.

"My existence is a comedy – those who invade my existence find tragedy."

"You would not threaten me – we go back too far – friends too long. I know you never really liked Greg: heck, the only time you and I ever had words was when I wouldn't fire the incompetent hack."

"Department of Redundancy Department! Incompetent hack – good one."

"You did the world a favor when you rid it of him. I was surprised you didn't get some time, but different states, different court systems, I'm glad you were spared."

"Spared? Methinks it had more to do with being in the right."

"And having the right lawyer."

"Let's kill all the lawyers – and let's do it today!"

"What about academicians? Don't we deserve to live and educate young minds like you did so well for so long?

"Methinks the gentleman doth protest too much."

"OK, this was cute to this point. Let me tell you why I came."

"Suicide wish?"

"No, I want you to head a new initiative the college is putting together. It's beyond anything colleges have ever done for writers – beyond the Iowa Writing Project, beyond Oxford, beyond Harvard, beyond anything anyone has done before for people who want to become writers. And we want you to head the program."

"Should I depart this kingdom I hath built, I should be considered a loggerheaded, bat-fowling dewberry."

"That's not a no. So you will think about it?"

"Ah, Romeo, Romeo, where hast thou mind gone, fair Romeo? For I am not your Juliet, but I shall walk among my minions like Richard V on the eve of battle, and make my decision henceforth."

With those words, Conrad began walking toward the A-frame. Jonathan Campbell hesitated, wondering how large a mistake he'd made and wondering how insane living alone drove his friend.

"I'm fine, by the way, Jonathan. Just putting you on like I always did. I'm not any more insane than anyone else. But as Buffett says, 'If we weren't all crazy, we'd go insane.'"

"That's a relief. You had me going there. Thought you'd gone over the deep end."

"Never been happier – never been more fulfilled. Isolation is by far the best thing I've ever done for myself; of course, it's about the first thing I ever did for myself. You'd be amazed at how marvelous all of this communing with nature is."

As the two approached, the feeding animals darted away from the A-frame, disallowing Conrad's hope of walking among them like Richard V. However, their departure answered the only question remaining – their leaving told him everything he needed to know.

"At least I didn't call you a tottering, motley-minded wagtail."

"No, thank you for sparing me that particular insult."

"Your favorite play still *Hamlet*?"

"The Olivier version. As I recall, we argued well Olivier versus Gibson."

"Olivier was much too old to play the young prince. Gibson was coming off the Mad Max movies, and was perfect for the part. One thing we agreed on: Branagh's version was much too long, too tedious, and only Crystal and Williams were effective in roles."

"To that, we definitely agree. Over five hours is way too long for any performance. Any chance you will resurrect your Hemingway show in the future?"

"Nope, done performing, except for the occasional slip into comedy when someone trespasses on my property."

"Do you get many trespassers?"

"You are the second."

"Greg..."

"The first and only; you see, people in this area are salt of the earth, and smart enough to take a blatant hint. No one comes to see me because these people, who don't have yours or Greg's high-powered Ph.Ds, are much smarter than any of us. Maybe it rests in the fact that their egos aren't as big as ours."

"Perhaps...how long do you need to give me an answer? Please say yes, because we know you are the perfect person to get this done."

"I'm not going to give you an answer today. But I do want you to do me one favor."

"Of course."

"No one does Hamlet's soliloquy better than you. Let me hear it."

Jonathan Campbell smiled and raised his shoulders, almost in triumph.

"To be or not to be..."

The sound of the gunshot silenced the soliloquy.

"Not to be…"

Chapter 12...Justice Remains Blind (or simply doesn't want to see)

No charges filed. After a lengthy conversation with various police entities, and an even longer discussion with the state attorney, determination came that it was the same case, same trial as before, and would invariably produce the same result. The cost of prosecuting outweighed the prosecutor's sense of justice.

"You do realize that what you're doing is wrong."

"Then prosecute me...charge me or let me go. With all due respect, these people come onto my property as trespassers and will continue to be treated as such. Now, the next time it happens, and it will probably happen at least one more time given the stupidity of the basic human being, let's be realistic. You took an oath to protect the citizens of this state; therefore, you need to keep them off my property. Perhaps some public service announcements on tv/radio/facadebook/twitter will help educate these people that I'm serious about no one trespassing."

"Well, Mr. Nevitt, I'm not going to prosecute you, and I'm not going to make a fool of myself on television telling people there's someone we have no control over and to stay away from him."

"Election's in six months – guess you don't need negative publicity."

"The election has nothing to do with it."

"With all due respect, and that's the second time I've used that phrase that we all know means no respect at all, it's all about politics. It's ok...it's the life you've chosen and apparently have done pretty well with. It appears that it's in everyone's best interest, politically and otherwise, to just leave me alone. You don't need another high-profile trial that you obviously won't win, which will give your opponent all the ammunition needed to beat you. I'm sure the press is outside now waiting for a statement. I'll give them a good one that makes you look good to voters. And that's what this is really all about."

The state prosecutor, Barney Barlow, sat back in his chair and thought about the words spoken by a man who had killed twice on his watch. However, the man became a sort of folk hero with the first – probably become a legend if he beats the second trial…and he would probably beat it. Plus, Nevitt was correct – losing a second such case would be damaging to Barlow's office and re-election.

"Alright, Mr. Nevitt, let's play your game. You beat us at ours, I'll give you that, so now let's see what happens when we play yours. But I don't care what you say to the press on your way out. Your support is not needed by this office."

"Well, I respect that, Mr. Barlow, and as my attorney once said to an aspiring candidate, I'll be for you or against you, whichever helps."

Barlow laughed out loud and acknowledged a good line.

"I'm not sure which it is in this case…but you're free to go. No charges."

Walking out of the office building, Conrad's prediction proved true and a number of local and state media besieged him, all wanting a statement.

"Members of the fifth or sixth or whatever estate we call journalism now, thank you for coming. The Honorable Mr. Barlow decided, in what I consider a wise and fair act, not to prosecute me for shooting a trespasser. The taxpayers lost a great deal of money that could be used for good when they tried to incarcerate me last time. I've done nothing wrong but protect my right to protect my property and my right to live in isolation. Mr. Barlow's decision, which by the way I agree with totally, saves the court system a great deal of time and money and allows it to do its work on people who should be prosecuted. I will not cause a backlog of cases this time. I am returning to my property and hope that, this time, humanity gets the message and you never have to take my picture or shoot video footage or write down the things I say again."

"Mr. Nevitt, if someone else comes on your property, will you shoot them?"

"If you have to ask that question, you obviously haven't been paying attention to anything, but I'll give you that it is a worthwhile question given the nature of your beast. So I'll answer the question. Anyone trespassing on my land will not leave. I will put a bullet in them – two or six if necessary. Whatever it takes. I simply want to be left alone and will take whatever means necessary to achieve my goal."

"Do you consider yourself a vigilante?"

"Hell, no...it's my property and myself I'm protecting. Look up the definition of vigilante and you'll realize how inane the question was, but I appreciate the question as a way of explaining I'm not out to hurt anyone – not my purpose. It's not the reason I shot two trespassers. The reason I shot them was they were trespassing and I want to be left alone. A vigilante seeks out guilty people and attacks them – I never seek out anyone. The only commonality I have with vigilante justice is the fact that, in normal cases, the vigilante starts out as a victim and turns the tables. Of course, I have been told there is a bit of resemblance with Charles Bronson. Maybe I should mumble my answers the rest of the interview."

"Some people are comparing you to Son of Sam, Charles Manson, or Ted Bundy. How do you respond to those people?"

"Well, that hurts, because those people killed for the simple thrill of murdering someone. I don't want to kill anyone, which takes me out of their circle. They killed because they wanted to, either out of some feeling of sick pleasure or some superiority complex, or the spectacle of it all. I shot two trespassers who had been warned in advance, and what makes it even sadder, both who were shot were warned specifically via e-mail not to come on my property. Guess it shows level of degree and level of intelligence don't necessarily go hand-in-hand."

"So, will you only shoot people who have Ph.D.s?"

Conrad's eyes and head dropped at perhaps the dumbest question he'd heard since a Super Bowl reporter asked quarterback Doug Williams how long he'd been a black quarterback, or a student of his asked Lambda Award-winning writer Fenton Johnson how long he'd been a gay writer. He search for a clever answer, but failed in the attempt.

"I shoot people to the degree that they are on my property."

"So it doesn't matter if they're college educated or not?"

"No, it could be you if you come on my property."

The reporter, Tom Howlett, seemed insulted by the comment, but then Conrad smiled, and the reporter smiled as well, realizing that, like the two dead men, he had it coming.

"By the way, sir, you know I was half-kidding, what's your name?"

"Tom Howlett, Mr. Nevitt. I'm with the *Pine City Daily News*."

"Oh, yeah, I read you guys online every morning."

"To see who died and who got arrested?" It was Howlett's turn to smile.

"Exactly – good one!"

For some reason, Conrad liked this reporter – a new experience. He hoped he never had to shoot him.

"I hope I never have to shoot you!"

"You have my word, sir, that I would never come on your property without an engraved, formal, perhaps even notarized invitation."

"I'll keep that in mind should I ever invite you."

"Would you?"

"I just might, but that would be some time in the distant future. Right now, I reiterate that I just want to be left alone. I will take one more question, but I'll take it only from Mr. Howlett."

"What does your utopian future hold?"

"Not bad – utopian…learn that in journalism school?"

"Got it from Dr. Larry Winn at Western Kentucky University."

"Great teacher."

"Something we have in common."

"Ah, you've done your homework to know something that trivial. Dr. Winn was one of my favorites and one of the reasons I got into that profession. When did you have him?"

"Right before he retired."

"He let you use any 'to be' verbs?"

"Loved his power verbs, Mr. Nevitt, but he would let me sneak in a was or were from time to time."

"He got soft in his old age – challenged us to never do it."

"Us, too, but I think he was ready to retire and tired of the bullshit we were full of."

"Right, I can identify. Now let me answer your question, Mr. Howlett. I'm nearing sixty-three years of age and for the past year, with just a couple of interruptions, have been able to live a life of solitude and isolation. So far, it's been everything positive imaginable. I don't see that changing anytime soon, but if it does, I'll make you a promise, and I seldom make promises, that you'll be the first to know if I change my mind about how I want to live."

"I am honored, Mr. Nevitt."

"Members of the press, as they used to say in the Mayberry of this state, and probably still do, 'you don't have to go home but you can't stay here.' I'm gone to Hank's Heaven."

The press conference ended.

Chapter 13...The Colors – the Pretty Colors

The fall proved everything Conrad expected. The leaves turned brilliant colors, the air channeled fresh, and the animals scurried about, obviously preparing for the inevitable change. Cellphone pictures abounded, as he downloaded each day the subtle changes in nature. His decision not to run away from technology within his isolation proved the correct choice – capturing and preserving these glorious images of God's gifts to the earth would bring pleasure each time recalled on the computer. So many of these lands were gone forever; Conrad nodded to himself each morning that the decision to preserve this land was the finest decision of his life.

No one entered his land this season.

The decision to isolate reinforced each morning when reading the various news services. Over the months, his reading list changed from the newspapers to the news services. Yahoo News caught his eye one day with its scroll of stories combining the various fields of news to which he was interested. The service appeared more fair and balanced than msn or fox; but then, how hard an achievement to be more fair and balanced than those two obviously biased sites? Everything from world to local, from entertaining and sports to the latest trends – written in clear, vivid prose – Yahoo News impressed him at a time when he never impressed. He found himself doing something he never found himself doing before: reading just one. Once in a while, he would glance at the others, but Yahoo News dominated his online reading.

Except for *The Pine City Daily News*. Obits, arrests, and Tom Howlett's stories claimed his attention every day, although Howlett's column appeared only twice a week. Otherwise, his bylines entailed hard news stories and investigations. Conrad liked the style, and was proud to know someone in the journalistic field who could actually write clear, concise sentences...and could actually spell words more than one syllable in length. His column inevitably contained collegiate-style prose.

I'll bet he's had more than one run-in with the editor about the language. While most of the paper is written for a middle-school reading level, columnists should be given more reign to write in a more educated style for the people who will actually read their column. Those of a middle-school reading level aren't going to read what Tom writes about. Glad my editor was like that.

Conrad reflected on the busiest time of his life – one where the many jobs included a weekly column on education. A smile crossed his face at the argument with editor Jeff regarding the word *plethora*. Conrad detested the term "a lot", believing it should only be used in terms of a piece of land. When Jeff demanded he change plethora to a lot, Conrad rewrote the column and inserted *myriad*. As always, the editor enjoyed the last word, and when the column appeared, the phrase "a bushel basket full" was the final answer. In the farming community, Conrad realized that might well indeed be the best way to say it. Jeff remained one of the few people in the world he trusted and one of the few with whom he continued to exchange communication. The editor and lifelong friend knew him well. Never, in any communication, did Jeff ask to get together. Jeff never visited or asked to visit.

He proved his intelligence.

After a light breakfast of a banana, Conrad strolled to the lounge chair, Ipad in hand. A skunk, nicknamed Baby Pewie, grazed at one of the bins. Thankful Pewie never got nervous around him, Conrad bid the polecat hello and sat. The two creatures understood that if one didn't bother the other, no bother would transpire. It had been that way for about six weeks since Baby Pewie first appeared, and Conrad hoped the relationship remained consistent. He noticed that the skunk always dined alone – a credit to the intelligence of the other animals, he assumed. The critter would dine for a few minutes, and then amble his way back into the woods. Only then would other creatures come out.

They proved their intelligence.

The scroll through Yahoo News showed the usual tension in the world, the idiocy of politics, and the latest who-screwed-who from Hollywood. An article titled "How Colleges are Turning Solid Citizens into Money-Crazed Adults" caught his eye, and he downloaded it immediately. The article was disappointing, simply stating the obvious and drowning itself in cliché after cliché about the learning process. The piece reminded him of the plethora (he grinned at the use of the word) of meetings attended that were simply re-statements of every meeting attended before. This article truly represented the Department of Redundancy Department. At the end, justification of his beliefs came about as he read about the author: a college president. He'd known several good ones in his day – been privileged to serve them as they proved able people in their jobs. There was Meredith Thomas, Huston Williams, and Beau Justice. Each were great to Conrad and each were excellent presidents. The one thing they all had in common is what virtually all college administrators have in common: no knowledge of classroom education. What separated these three were they knew they didn't understand the

79

classroom – only Williams ever taught a class, and he did that simply to see what it was like and try to gain an understanding.

After the semester was over, President Williams apprised the faculty, "You have no idea how much respect I have for you folks now."

Illumination is a great trait. Conrad wagered the writer of the article never graced a classroom since completing his Ph.D. With time and curiosity on his side, a Google-search validated his hypothesis. There was no record of the writer ever teaching a class. But, he was an expert on the college classroom experience.

Now that he succeeded in urinating himself off about academia, Conrad called up *The Pine City Daily News*. The feature story was a murder-suicide – those were becoming so prominent he wondered if these were even newsworthy anymore. The story on this one was so blurred they weren't sure whether he shot her and then himself or she shot him and then herself. The bottom line was they both were dead.

Today's arrest report also included a familiar name. A drug raid resulted in a series of arrests, including the familiar name. Conrad shook his head – must be the fifth or sixth time over the years this person was arrested. Each time, money exchanged hands and little time was served. This time, a DUI charge added to the list of offenses. The family succeeded each time in securing the minimum penalty.

How many times is enough before they realize this problem child/adult needs to go away? I wish one time this person would visit...

Conrad became irritated that it bothered him. After all, this person was none of his business, none of his affair, not any part of his life. No sense in letting blood pressure skyrocket over a trivial human being.

Looking around, Conrad realized his obliviousness to the menagerie. Every food bin was occupied, with the usual cast of suspects: turkeys, groundhogs and possum. Each ate well, and he hoped the animals were ingesting the health-enhancing drugs along with the food. The internet veterinarian made no promises for the success of these new drugs, but they were worth a try if they bettered the health of at least a few creatures. Conrad followed the vet's instructions to the letter and had sent her detailed descriptions of the animals over the past two months. Everyone seemed healthy and several, including Baby Pewie, looked their best today with additional weight needed for winter survival.

Reading list done and animals fed, Conrad veered off the schedule in deciding not to fish today. The woods beckoned, and a simple walk up the hillside past the cabin to the top of Hank's Heaven seemed appropriate. Besides, he hadn't inspected the second pond (the second pond needed a better name) but once or twice since arriving.

The second of the three ponds Hank built last and basically carved it out of a hill. It sat a couple hundred yards at an angle above the small pond (which truly needed a name), and held more fish per square foot than either of the other ponds. Logically the case, because of the three, it was seldom fished because of all the brush and briarpatches Hank left surrounding the water. If one wanted ticks on their body, the second pond was the place to go. The few times Conrad fished it, he spent minutes spraying himself down with deep forest repellent, and still, when showering, would find one or two of the little demons attached to his body. He caught nice bass and crappie each time, but the catch wasn't worth the hassle – especially when two ponds with easier access produced great quality fish. Perhaps that was Hank's reason for building the second pond in the first place – one area that would remain unspoiled. Conrad liked that idea.

As he walked the trail toward the top of the knob, he paused when parallel to the second pond. Picture-resistance was futile, so the cellphone came out and several angles were shot. This pond represented natural habitat and Conrad wasn't sure he would bother it again.

The trail constructed by Hank years ago remained virtually intact despite lack of trailblazing. Conrad seldom came this way on his daily walks – too much uphill climb for his taste. But once in a while, he liked to venture to the top of the knob and sit on the jutting-edged rock at the top. He always liked the term "Master of his domain" until the sitcom *Seinfeld* ruined it – that show Conrad considered the most over-rated television show of all time.

Whiney New Yorkers would have made an appropriate title.

While walking, his thoughts turned to all those sitcoms watched through the years. He liked to think through his favorites:

- *Mash: Loved Hawkeye, Klinger, Father Mulcahy, and both Colonels*
- *Leave it to Beaver: My childhood*
- *Modern Family: downright funny*

- *The Andy Griffith Show: always called it The Barney Fife Show...wasn't as good without old Don Knotts*

- *All in the Family: Archie changed the way we looked at the world*

- *Two and a Half Men: Charlie was a train wreck but fun to watch a train wreck. Funny my favorite characters were all women (Evelyn, Berta and Rose)*

- *The Drew Carey Show: any show with Ryan Stiles was funny*

- *Mary Tyler Moore: Ted was a hoot, and Rhoda should have been on Seinfeld, but Sue Ann Nivens cracked me up. Hell, Betty White always cracks me up no matter what she does*

- *South Park: those little foul-mouthed bastards seldom failed to make me laugh...and think about the issues they lampooned*

- *The Simpsons: Love the article on Yahoo News that says my generation would be studied sociologically by studying episodes of this show – they tackled everything*

- *Married...with Children: Al Bundy...the end.*

He remembered his Mom talking about Al Bundy and that show as the nastiest, worst thing she ever saw...and she tuned in every Sunday night and laughed.

Conrad stopped for a breather, having walked within about thirty yards of the knob's peak. Reaching into his Tampa Bay Rays' backpack, orange Gatorade quenched his thirst, as it had for years. Some people were alcoholics, some were drug addicts – he was a Gatoradist. Couldn't drink enough of it. At least, no studies were found that it was a cancer-causing drink, but he surmised that study would come out at any time. All those years drinking sodas should have left him dead by now, but perhaps all the coffee and tea he drank offset them.

Everything in moderation; nothing to excess.

He lived life by that mantra, and his children, students, and acquaintances must have heard his voice utter those words a million times. It seemed every new study contradicted the past one. This is good, this is not good, this is okay, this is bad, this is bad...good cholesterol, bad cholesterol, then good was bad and bad was good. Red meat bad – red meat needed; coffee bad, whoops, coffee in moderation good.

Everything in moderation; nothing to excess.

The peak reached, Conrad sat on the jagged-edge rock and looked out over the panoramic view. Into his sightline came both The Big Lake and The Small Pond (both in dire need of names), but he couldn't see the second lake (it probably didn't want one in order to keep its anonymity). The cabin and the A-frame remained visible but seemed so small from this venue – like the Earth from the Moon and beyond. The one site he used to hate no longer made the list of despised things: the interstate highway. There was actually some comfort in knowing civilization was that close by, and a great deal of satisfaction that civilization no longer consumed him.

Isolation was attained.

Silence...wonderful silence...cars and trucks on the interstate too far to be heard...peace and serenity abounded.

...until a low growl broke the silence.

Chapter 14...A Man's Got to Know his Limitations

Conrad turned to view the big cat standing about 20 yards away in a small opening which led to the northeast corner of the property. Pondering a moment, Conrad realized in all these years, never once had he ventured to that portion of Hank's Heaven. The reason simple: there was no water in that portion so no need to go. Exploring for exploring's sake never enticed him – fishing was his thing, so water was his deal. Besides, the topology of the property revealed boring details for Conrad's universe, so he left that part of the universe alone. The fact that the topology of that particular area revealed ideal conditions for such creatures as diamondback rattlesnakes might reveal a clue as to why he never explored the northeast corner.

He did not fear snakes – he respected them greatly. One of his first experiences as a child here was exploring a barn near The Big Lake; of course he explored, it was the only place his grandfather made off limits to him. The seven year-old realized quickly the error of his ways when the largest reptile he'd seen in his young life appeared in the opposite corner of the barn. If someone had been behind him, young Conrad was sure he would have run over them regardless of their size. The proof was there – Hank's teenage son was indeed behind him and, indeed, Conrad knocked the teenager to the ground on his way to apologize to his grandfather and promise never to disobey ever, ever again.

Minutes later, Hank's son emerged from the barn holding the head and body of the now-deceased rattler, and for years, the outside of the barn displayed the preserved snakeskin. Conrad wasn't sure if the display was to frighten anyone trespassing, or to simply tell rattlers what would happen to them if caught in the barn. To Conrad's knowledge, no rattlesnake had ever been spotted near the southeast corner again, but Hank and others who hiked in the northeast corner always had at least one diamondback story to tell upon their return.

Guess they all got the message or read the manual!

Realizing his daydream was probably not the brightest time for one, given the big cat's continued presence a short distance away, Conrad placed his gaze back on the big cat.

"Hey, Big Cat, how the hell are you?"

He realized watching all those John Wayne movies caused him to use the Duke's voice now. He hoped to have Duke's luck in winning battles.

The Big Cat stared like he was sizing up the situation for any danger to himself. Conrad felt the animal change his eyeline from the eyeball to eyeball to the human's hip.

"Oh, you see the glock, huh? Now, let's get this straight. I like you, I respect you, and I will leave your ass alone as long as you don't screw with me. But I am not going to take any chances and I will shoot you if you attack."

Conrad quickly patted the gun twice and raised his right arm parallel to his shoulder, trying to send a message to the creature that the next-to-last thing he wanted to happen was to shoot The Big Cat. Of course, the last thing he wanted to happen was to be attacked.

Oddly, The Big Cat seemed, perhaps to Conrad's imagination, amused by the scene. The creature almost possessed a mocking countenance that conveyed he didn't take the human seriously about anything.

So Conrad laughed, sharing the amusement.

"OK, so I'm not a badass like you. What's you gonna do, Big Boy? Again, he patted the gun and raised his arm."

An even lower growl met his ears, and The Big Cat turned and trotted through the forest toward the northeast corner.

"Guess you know I'm not going to follow your ass in there, don't you."

Another growl, just loud enough to be audible. No anger discernible in the growl left Conrad believing the two reached an understanding. He might own the entire property line, but the northeast corner was The Big Cat's domain.

No problem.

Conrad surveyed the beauty one last time for this day. The interstate seemed especially traffic-congested, which made him all the more appreciative of his decision-making skills. He looked up to thank God, as he did every day several times, and noticed cloud formations shifting – including one darker than the others appearing to head toward the knob top.

Time to go.

But not before pausing to say the prayer his grandfather taught him years ago. He thought it was the prayer of St. Francis – wasn't sure whether it was St. Francis of Assisi, St. Francis of Amanly, or St. Francis Xavier – but relatively sure it was one of the St. Francises:

God, grant me the serenity to accept the things I cannot change, the courage to change the things I can, and the wisdom to know the difference.

Conrad wasn't sure the words were exact, but didn't care – the prayer mattered. Whether or not God existed, Conrad remained devoted to the prayer, saying it several times a day. Whenever he did, he felt better. And he couldn't argue with the gifts received over the course of his lifetime. He remained thankful to whatever deity existed. Organized religion dominated the first part of his life. Altar boy, lector, Eucharistic minister, parish council member, Conrad knew the Catholic Church well. He was never ashamed of his religion, despite telling students on opening day of classes that he was "part of the most corrupt institution the world has ever known: Catholicism." Every organized religion was human-instigated and operated; therefore, every organized religion was flawed. Conrad loved the principles of the Catholic Church – he just wished they would practice what they preached.

As old Twain said, "Money is not the root of all evil. Lack of money is the root of all evil." The Church enjoyed more money that any single entity, and he remembered his fallout. The sexual scandal did not cause his self-excommunication – it was the handling of it. When the Church forbade priests from marriage (an 11th century decree, if he recalled his church history correctly), the priesthood became a haven for gay men and pedophiles to escape the real world. Granted, the overwhelming majority of priests, especially those he knew, were wonderful men dedicated to doing the right thing. In all his childhood of being an altar boy for countless masses, funerals and weddings, not one of the dozens of priests he knew ever made any overture toward him.

I must have been a really ugly kid.

He knew that wasn't true, but never let the truth get in the way of a good story. In all, only one priest he knew ever ran afoul of the church, and that was not because he was a pedophile – he was simply a gay priest who "whet his sexual appetite" with other men. When it was discovered, his fate was similar to the pedophiles – a simple relocation to another assignment.

That was where Conrad disagreed with the Catholic Church. Reassignment? What good did that do? All that did was wipe the slate clean and allow them to find more victims. As a teacher/administrator at a Catholic university, and having published several articles ripping the Church for the reassignment practice, he felt that he had not sat idly by – that he attacked the problem the way a good Christian should (good Christian not necessarily being either a redundancy or an oxymoron). His leaving the university in mid-semester was not the result of the articles or pressure from the college or church authorities. It was much simpler than that:

A university offered twice his salary for him to move…Duh!

His falling out came after back to back mass attendance, one at his hometown cathedral and the other in his new hometown. On successive Sundays, two priests, who could not have been more different in background, generation, and philosophy, gave the same homily: Parishioners needed to tithe especially to assist in paying attorneys' fees for the defense of those priests accused of these crimes.

WTF?

The unmitigated audacity of the Church proved too much for Conrad – ask him to pay for them to get off (pun intended) when the Church reassigned these criminals to other parishes knowing these people could and would commit the crimes again? It was too much. Conrad remembered getting out of his pew in mid-homily and barking aloud:

"The Catholic Church does not deserve a fan like me. The hypocrisy of the last two homilies I've heard is too much for me to bear. To stay with the church would make me as huge a hypocrite as the people who run it. Martin Luther remains correct."

Since that day, Conrad Nevitt never graced a Catholic Church. He wondered if it was just the one religion, but then started reading accounts of other denomination leaders who fell from grace for various reasons, such as embezzlement, alcoholism, pedophilia, and even a local religious leader who was arrested for stealing condoms from Wal-Mart.

Organized religion became a pariah to Conrad, and while he remained loving of the deity and remained devoted to doing things the Christian way, he found a new and better way to worship. He found God in the best place to find Him: his own heart and Hank's Heaven.

While most people would assume the hike back an easier trek, Conrad detested downhill walking. He tended to go too fast and tended to fall due to failure to watch his own steps. However, this time he trod more carefully, probably because he felt The Big Cat's eyes on him and did not want to give the animal further cause for amusement. Falling on his face was not going to happen this time.

But it did anyway.

Lost in his thoughts about organized religion, Conrad leaned forward a bit too far and lost his footing, tumbling head over heels for a few feet downhill. He caught himself and immediately performed self-inventory on his physique. A twinge in his left shoulder told him there was a slight injury there along with a couple of scratches on his left arm. He always managed to fall on his left side, probably due to protecting his stronger, right side. Otherwise, he seemed fine. Knees functioned properly, back didn't appear worse for wear, and his head was as clear as it could be given all the clutter of sixty-two and a half years. His steps remained firm, and he walked more upright the remainder of the way.

When he reached the cabin, he noticed the twinge in his left shoulder continued. Opening the door, he strode to the couch, stopping at the refrigerator on the way to pluck the icepack from the freezer. Lowering to the couch, the twinge became a sharp pain, and he wondered if he'd done any permanent damage to an area of his body that had never been hurt. The icepack felt good, but the pain remained. He moved the collar of his polo shirt to inspect further, and saw a bruise already forming – not a good sign.

The pink light on the monitor blinked. Someone entered the southeast corner.

Chapter 15...Third Time Not Necessarily a Charm

Surprised at someone entering the least accessible area of Hank's Heaven, Conrad wondered if this trespasser presented a danger. The first two trespassers incorrectly relied on friendship keeping them alive, and paid for their stupidity.

Ph.Ds don't change the fact they're dead. Dead is dead. They were warned.

This felt different. Whomever this was took a much longer and much more difficult route to get on the property – there was no road access. If they came from the interstate, they bypassed the other entrances and made their way through thick forest to get on the property in the worst place possible. If they came from the front of the property and moved to that place, same thing. The only other way was to have come through the private preserve adjacent to Hank's Heaven, and that would take time and utmost effort to cross those knobs and get through property that, to Conrad's knowledge, no one had ever walked. Even Hank, in his youth, left that area alone, saying it was "too damn thick and dangerous for a man of my abilities." It was the most difficult of all the signs to place, and Conrad nearly left the area be, thinking no one fool enough to cross there.

But his thoroughness got the best of him and he struggled, macheted, and finally got the sign and monitor in place. He used the pinklight designation simply because it was another color in the spectrum and he felt it would never go off.

Wrong again.

As Conrad continued in a southeasterly direction, a human image came into view. He raised his rifle and locked in on the target, bound and determined to keep his vow of shooting anyone and everyone who trespassed. The sight locked, moments from pulling the trigger, he paused.

He refused to kill a child, especially one on her knees in tears.

Looking around for other trespassers, Conrad closed on her position. Her wailing increased as she was oblivious to his presence, so he closed another ten yards before calling.

"Young lady, who the hell are you and what the hell are you doing here?"

Slowly, eyes lacking life peered at him, and in one breathless tone she exclaimed, "Please kill me...please shoot! I don't want to go on anymore."

"Tell me who you are."

"My name's not important...I'm not important...I want to die...fire the gun!"

Conrad closed to within a few feet, but backed away when the girls lunged for the gun. Still, he did not shoot. Curiosity killed a cat, but his curiosity would not let him kill this girl – yet.

"I will ask again: who are you?"

"If I tell you, will you go ahead and pull the trigger?"

"Probably."

"Then I am Morgan. Now shoot."

"I lied, Morgan. Come with me."

Morgan rose and he could see she was somewhere in her early teens, but age was not something he'd ever judged well. She reeked of body odor and the mess that passed for clothes looked like she'd been through several trials and tribulations to reach this point.

"Before I decide what to do, tell me how you got here."

"I ran away and have been running for several days. I don't know how many. I'm tired and I'm hungry and I'm hurting and I just wish you would put me out of my hurt. Please, shoot!"

"Maybe later."

Conrad held out his hand, deciding not to kill for the moment. His rationale was that she wasn't trespassing, and his vow was to shoot trespassers. That was his story and he was sticking to it – for the time being. With easy-to-discern trepidation, the girl took his hand, allowed him to help her to her feet, and the two walked back to the A-frame. No words were exchanged on the walk. Once at the A-frame door, Conrad made a decision.

"Inside you will find a shower with soap and towels, and there is a bag in the bedroom closet where you will find clothes that will be a bit big, but at least are clean. Leave your clothes on the floor of the bathroom and I will wash them. I'll be out here when you're done and we'll see about getting you something to eat. But first, you stink and you need to get clean."

"I don't know whether to cuss you out or say thank you."

"Don't say either until you mean one or the other and we'll get along fine. Don't lie to me and don't provoke me. Still haven't decided what's going to happen, but if you do what I tell you, you might make it through the day. Might. Oh, by the way, if you run, I will shoot you in the leg – that hurts real bad, so don't do it. I don't want to have to take a knife and cut into your leg to get my damned bullet back, understand?"

"Yeah."

"I'll be over here." Conrad motioned to his lounge chair. He noticed no animals were around, obviously spooked by Morgan's presence and countenance.

About forty-five minutes passed before she came out of the A-frame, wearing some basketball shorts he'd grown out of years ago but hadn't thrown away due to sentimental value, and wearing a Rays' shirt that was fairly old – the letters "Crawford" were across the back, signifying the first Tampa Bay baseball star, Carl Crawford. He hadn't played for the team in years.

Morgan sat at the foot of his lounge chair and immediately asked, "What do you plan to do with me?"

"Feed you and send you on your way."

"You're not going to shoot me? But you're the Lord Protector of Hank's Heaven."

"How do you know that?"

"When I was in the shower, I realized I had seen this place before…on the news on my Daddy's television. I read about you in the newspaper in that Howlett guy's story. You're some kind of famous, aren't you?"

"More infamous than famous, and if you knew I was around, why were you stupid enough to come onto my property?"

"I want to commit suicide but I'm scared to do it myself. Thought by coming on your property, you'd do it for me."

"So you are trespassing? Dammit to hell! Tell me you wandered aimlessly onto my property. Tell me that now."

"You told me not to lie to you."

Conrad liked the quick thinking, but now, because of this revelation, had to re-think and re-rationalize not killing her.

"How old are you?"

"Fourteen."

New rule: don't kill anyone under 18. There, he successful rationalized.

"Let's walk up to cabin. I've got some food up there."

"P B and J? That's my favorite."

"We'll see and you'll take what I give you."

It bothered Conrad a bit how quickly she brightened from earlier in the day, and thoughts turned to being conned so many times by people. Thoughts of killing re-entered but he would let this drama play out for a little while.

Morgan consumed three sandwiches in such a manner as Conrad knew food hadn't crossed her path in a while. She gulped down the Gatorade so quickly she seemed to choke a couple of times, but each time, righted herself and continued the meal. No questions asked, as he felt it best to let her enjoy something before any decisions were made.

Moving to the couch, the cross-examination began.

"All right, little girl, tell me your story, and don't lie to me. I might have put the rifle away, but my trusty gluck remains by my side."

Thinking she caught him by surprise, Morgan bounded out the door in a flash and began to move down the path. Conrad anticipated her bolting, and followed just as quickly out the door, pulling his glock in speed old west gunfighters would have admired.

BANG!

The bullet grazed her leg and Morgan grasped it immediately, falling to the ground believing she was in more pain than she actually was.

"You shot me!"

"Told you I would, and I'm a man of my word. The only difference was I didn't lodge the bullet in your leg – only grazed it. You should have something that looks like a little cut with some blood oozing but nothing serious. I don't feel like extracting a bullet so don't run again.

Next time, I WILL put the bullet in your leg. Now, get up, get your ass back in the cabin, we'll fix that leg up and you can tell me your true story."

Morgan whimpered but only a bit. She gave him a quizzical look as she passed him on the return walk to the cabin.

Settled back onto the couch, treatment on the leg began. The small cut required only some rubbing alcohol and a band-aid.

"I'm a helluva good shot, don't you think?"

"You shot me."

"I'm betting that's not the worst thing that's happened to you recently and, besides, I could kill you or worse."

"I've had worse."

"I figured as much. Let's hear it."

"No. Kill me."

"I'll do worse than that. I'll tie your ass to the first gate and call authorities to come and get you. Then you'll spend a couple of days telling them your story or you can tell me and we can decide what to do from there."

"I'll take my chances with you."

"Smart girl."

"But I would like a favor before telling the story."

"Demanding, huh? Well, what are your demands?"

"I would like one of the Pepsis from the fridge."

Conrad snorted and retrieved the beverage.

"Guess you demand that I open it for you as well."

"If you're a gentleman..."

Conrad opened the beverage.

"Everything was great. Lots of love from Mom and Dad, school was fun and I was a real good student, and I had a little bother who bugged me but I loved him anyway."

"You mean brother."

"No, he was a bother. He was Dad's from another woman and Mom took him in as her own. She was better about it than I was, but she forgave Dad, so I did too...so we both forgave him. Then he did it again – knocked up this cheap slut so Mom kicked him out. We got along good for a while until she started seein' this guy that was really bad news. He hated my little bother and I from the get-go and we hated him. No matter how hard we tried to get Mom to get rid of him, they just got closer and she asked him to move in with us. That was awful. He was so mean to us. He'd beat the bother and then he started comin' into my room late and night smellin' of the funny stuff."

"OK, that's enough. I get the picture. Can't blame you for leaving."

"You ain't heard the worst."

"Don't need to – heard enough. You can stay in the A-frame for a day or two before doing whatever it is you need to do. You can't stay here for long – they'll find you and take you back."

"Oh my God!"

"What?"

"I've lost Mom's wedding ring. It's the only thing I have of hers. I got to find it."

A search of the cabin, the A-frame, and the grounds surrounding the A-frame came up empty. So they retraced their steps back to the southeast corner where she entered.

"You fell right here. I remember and there's a bit of torn cloth in the spot."

Morgan picked up the tattered cloth. Underneath it, in the midst of a tuft of grass, laid the shiny object they searched for.

"I am so happy. I can't lose this. It's all I have of hers."

"You'll see her again."

"No...I won't...thank you for your kindness and thank you for not shooting me but once in the leg. I got to be going."

"You should get some rest."

"Can't rest...got to keep going. I'm heading the interstate to hitchhike as far away from here as possible. But thank you."

Morgan kissed Conrad's cheek and he directed her to the corner where the interstate was closest. He wished her good luck.

She disappeared quickly. He trudged through the brush over to the fence so that the monitor could be re-set. In all the excitement, he'd forgotten to do that and was now upset with himself to ever forget such an important act. Reaching out, he hit the re-set button and the pink color began glowing again. However, his eyes caught a glare on an object below. Taken a bit by surprise, he reached into his pocket for a paper towel he always kept there for emergencies. He leaned down and, using the paper towel, picked up the object that caused him great consternation.

It was a 45-calibre pistol, and it appeared to have been recently fired...twice.

Chapter 16...It's in the Paper – It must be True

The gun placed in the drawer adjacent to his bed in the cabin, Conrad wondered what the girl shot. Two chambers empty, perhaps she fired one to see what it felt like, and the second to be sure. Relieved she left, Conrad nearly forgot his nightly routine.

Tap! Turn...lie down. He and The Big Cat continued the ritual.

Gallaraga! A great, majestic name for his friend.

The name for The Big Cat should never have taken this long – too easy once realized. He named the creature after one of his favorite baseball players, Andres Gallaraga, nicknamed The Big Cat. An excellent player, Gallaraga hung around years past his prime due to work ethic, leadership, and personality. He was an outstanding mentor/teacher to young ballplayers, and led by example. Literature background kicked in, tying his feelings for the animal to Santiago's feelings for the marlin in *The Old Man and The Sea*. Even in capture, the respect for the beast elevated each day, and the sadness permeated throughout the old man when the inevitable death resulted. So many references to The Great DiMaggio in Hemingway's work – baseball a common theme to both the great writer and now, the great loner.

Conrad smiled, not knowing whether he just complimented or insulted himself, or simply compared himself to one of the great writers of all time, which could still be construed as a compliment or an insult. He was nothing like Papa...yet yes he was. For so many years, audiences were needed – the need to have people around constantly consumed his life. Boisterous and humorous in a crowd, hard-drinking and hard-living for many years, perhaps Conrad subconsciously lived the Hemingway style.

He recalled fondly his first of many trips to Key West. Sloppy Joe's Tavern earned must-see status, and his first visit taught him how little he truly knew about the man he thought well researched.

"Hello, sir, I can certainly see why you're here."

"Really? I just came in for a drink and to sit at the bar where Mr. Hemingway reportedly sat and held court on multiple occasions."

"Aren't you here for the contest? If you aren't, you should be."

"I can't say yes to the question, because I haven't a clue what contest you're talking about."

"The Hemingway lookalike contest...you really don't know. You look just like him with that gray hair and gray beard with round face. Not quite as good looking a man as Mr. Hemingway, though, but you could win the contest."

"There went your tip! No, seriously, I'm not here for that – just here to see where he hung out and get a feel for the place."

"Well, if you change your mind, we have the entry forms here. Go look at the wall and see the past winners – you'll see you look more like him that all but maybe a couple of them – and you look as much like him as they do. Oh, you would need to do some small act to portray him."

"I could probably do that should I decide to enter."

Much of Conrad's life was spent performing as Hemingway. Thirteen states, if confusion was counted as one, were included in the various tours. How had he missed knowing about this contest in all his research? He laughed, knowing no one is as smart as they think they are.

Especially writers. People seldom understood writers were people, too. All possessed their demons; for some, those demons made them great writers: Poe, Nelson, Cash, Kerouac, Thompson, and Morrison. Hemingway must have been bi-polar, perhaps tri-polar, maybe just multi-polar, but mood swings are mood swings and he had 'em by the boatload. Modern medicine might have saved him, but probably would have killed him given how many expensive pills would have been prescribed. Ah, those self-proclaimed feminazis I worked with once upon a time hated Hemingway so much, wanting to kick him out of the canon, and not kick him in the ass – the other side preferred. They got so mad at me defending him in that graduate class with Dr. Heldman. Hemingway didn't chase women – he let them chase him, and let the rich ones catch him. Oh, God, they got so mad at that...but none of the beeyotches had any evidence to the contrary, and it managed to shut 'em up for the moment.

Getting back in focus, Conrad remembered strongly considering entrance to the contest. He went back to the Keys annually right before the Hemingway celebration, but never remained long enough to enter. It wasn't fear of losing; rather, the Keys were a refuge away from it all. His lifetime experienced one competition after another – sometimes multiple competitions at once. The Keys constituted his first-ever true oasis other than Hank's Heaven. Rules applied only by him to him, and whatever rules applied, he followed. They prepared him effectively for what he experienced now: solitude and isolation. The Keys provided transition for him, helping him realize more and more control over his surroundings – a place to experiment with isolation and a place where people could be found easily – people never to be seen again. It seemed he stayed longer with each visit.

The Keys deserved many gratitudes, for each visit further prepared him for Hank's Heaven…

The next morning, the headline and sub-heading in *The Pine City Daily News* reached out from the screen and smacked Conrad across the temple.

Suicide Dropped from Murder-Suicide Belief

Woman's daughter prime suspect in double-shooting

The picture carried with the story made Conrad sit upright in the lounge chair. No doubt the picture was the girl from yesterday.

Dammit to hell!

Conrad knew what should be done, but hated doing it. The last thing wanted reared its ugly head. Little doubt her trail would be tracked through Hank's Heaven, so little use in waiting. Proactive much better than reactive here, and perhaps he could control how he was used if he went ahead and sent them everything he knew in an e-mail. Do it right away before any control lost.

Calling his e-mail, conradhemingway@yahoo.com, he searched for Tom Howlett's address. Carefully, he composed a near-thorough account of yesterday's events, including her hitchhiking southbound on the interstate. The one thing he failed to mention was the gun. He wasn't sure why he left that out, but told himself he would avail of the gun should anyone ask. Great pains were taken to deflect any possible wrongdoing on Conrad's part, emphasizing he possessed absolutely no knowledge of the girl other than she was an obvious runaway with a sad story. He drafted several versions until satisfied police couldn't make any more out of the story than what was actually there, and trying to ensure no further questions were necessary.

At the end of the communique, Conrad asked Howlett to print the e-mail, take it to the police, and apprise them everything he knew was in there – no need to come out to Hank's Heaven…there was nothing to add.

He went about reading other things on the internet, periodically returning to the e-mail to see if Howlett answered. After about twenty minutes, the replay came.

"Thank you, Mr. Nevitt, for the account. I am greatly honored you had enough faith in me to contact me and I will try to handle things in accordance with your wishes. I have a meeting with my editor right away on the matter, but I assure you I will be turning this over to the police. However, you must have assumed I would print your e-mail in the paper sometime in the next couple of days. As a former member of our profession, I'm sure you already knew we'd do that – it is the only true purpose of the newspaper business: to sell newspapers. If I can ever be of help to you again in any way, please do not hesitate to contact me."

Actually, Conrad never thought about his letter being printed, having hastily thought the matter through. Still, he didn't deem it a problem. Howlett's comment about the purpose of the newspapers amused thoroughly. Two questions always on his journalism exam: What is the primary goal of newspapers? What is the primary goal of television/radio news?

To sell newspapers and to obtain high ratings were the only acceptable answers.

Naptime was interrupted by a cellphone ring, the first call received in quite some time. For some reason, Conrad glanced at the number, although he certainly was not going to answer. One of his steadfast rules was that one never had to answer a ringing phone. If it's important enough, the person leaves a message.

After the ringing stopped, he waited for the familiar bing that signaled a message left. Several seconds later, the bing sounded. No surprise at the message:

"Mr. Nevitt, we are sorry to bother you, but this is Deputy Sheriff Ted Hahn, and we are investigating the apparent murder of Lawrence and Beverly Jones. We understand you have information concerning our lead suspect, Miss Catherine Smith, and would appreciate a call back. We understand your dedication to privacy, Mr. Nevitt, so a phone call could keep us from coming out there. Thank you. The number is 1-800-333-2222."

Conrad wrote down the number although didn't feel it necessary giving the ease with which that number could be remembered. He realized the sooner he called, the sooner this would be over and calling right away sent the proper signal of cooperation, along with the hope the authorities would determine no need to enter the property.

"Sheriff's Department...to whom may I direct your call?"

"I am returning Deputy Hahn's call. This is Conrad Nevitt."

"Thank you, so nice of you, Mr. Nevitt, for returning Deputy Hahn's call. I will forward you to his phone."

"Thank you."

"Ted Hahn."

"Conrad Nevitt, Deputy Hahn."

"Thank you, so nice of you, Mr. Nevitt for returning my call."

Obviously, telephone etiquette was passed with flying colors, and the cookie-cutter method often is the best.

"This call is a courtesy call, Deputy, for as I stated in the e-mail, I told you everything I knew and follow-up was unnecessary."

"My apologies, Mr. Nevitt, but our procedures make follow-up standard protocol. I will try to make this as brief and painless as possible."

"That would be in everyone's best interest."

The two discussed the contents of the communique and further discussed Conrad's impressions of the girl's demeanor. The conversation lasted nearly an hour but appeared to leave the Deputy satisfied all that could be said had been said.

"We truly appreciate you taking time to return my call, Mr. Nevitt. We are fully aware of your dedication to isolation, and have made every effort to ensure you are left alone. We hope you understand an exception needed to be made in this particular case."

"Actually, I do realize that, and it's why I returned the call. You weren't the only exception made in this particular case."

"And what is that, Mr. Nevitt?"

"I didn't shoot her – she's the only person who has trespassed onto my property who was allowed to leave still standing. Not sure if it was the right thing to do but I made the exception and I'll live with it."

"You realize if we don't find her in the next 48 hours, we'll get a warrant and search your property."

"Don't like the tone of that, Deputy Hahn. So let me give you a tone: Don't make the mistake of coming onto the property. She left. If I had shot her, I would tell you because we both know there would be no prosecution of me coming, and I never want to worry about disposing of bodies. I told the prosecutor I'd always let you know when someone was shot so that you could come get them. She was alive and well and headed for the interstate the last time I saw her."

"Is there anything else to add to our conversation?"

"Just to reiterate my warning to the good people in law enforcement that they will be considered trespassers if entering my property."

"We would have a warrant."

"Warrants are great, but remember what a wise person told me years ago: Dead is dead."

"I understand, Mr. Nevitt. I will do everything in my power to ensure you are left alone."

"That's in everybody's best interest. Good luck catching her. She seems quite resourceful, but then, children enduring what she endured often become the most resourceful humans."

"We thank you for your time, Mr. Nevitt."

"Good day."

What's this we shit? I hate when people say we and there's no one else around. Guess there's always someone else to blame when "we" is used – no one ever wants personal responsibility for anything anymore. I hope "we" find her or I hope "we" understand the consequences of entering Hank's Heaven – warrant or not – I won't care.

We protect our own...

Chapter 17...Winter Makes Strange Bedfellows

The possibility of a law enforcement invasion became moot when the girl was discovered in Gulf Shores, Alabama. Turned out to be a bad move on her part, as a number of people in the town nearest Hank's Heaven owned condominiums on the water in the deep south. Catherine Smith succeeded in passing herself off as old enough to wait tables, but suffered the misfortune of working a table of people familiar with the story from *The Pine City Daily News*. A quick notification to local police resulted in quick extradition and transport back to stand trial. Because of her youth, the prosecutor was reluctant to try her as an adult, but political pressure won out.

Conrad wondered if he would be subpoenaed, and wondered who would possess enough balls to try and serve the document. He prepared for the inevitable, but sometimes the inevitable turns another path.

Catherine's attorney turned out to be Conrad's old friend, Goldstein, and thus knew better than to summon his former client. J.D. never failed to pick the right card from his sleeve, and after careful jury selection, played the abuse, neglect and other horrible treatment imposed on a minor. The old "he had it coming" defense expanded to "they had it coming."

The prosecution never had a chance.

Not guilty. Evidence failed to overcome emotion once again in this state's jurisdiction.

Reading daily transcripts of the trial amused Conrad, and he delighted in the fact that Tom Howlett received the assignment. The more he read Howlett's work, the better he liked it.

If I ever do my memoirs, I'll get Howlett to write them...if I don't do them myself.

After the trial ended, Conrad's reading produced one comment he didn't see coming. In her statement to the press following acquittal, 14 year-old Catherine Smith stated:

"I want to thank everyone who came to my defense during this awful thing. I had a great defender who I will always think the world of, but I want to thank most of all Conrad Nevitt. If he hadn't done what he did, I don't think I would have gotten my head together. His kindness in taking care of me that day gave me hope again. I thank him for sparing me, even though he did shoot me in the leg. Everybody goes on his property gets shot, and I wasn't no exception. But he didn't kill me, and I know it was hard for him not to. I know he reads the papers on his computer, so I hope he'll know I thank him for what he done. I hope he's happy and I hope y'all keep leavin' him alone – that's all he wants...and that's all I want now...just leave me be."

Mixed emotions filled Conrad. He wasn't sure what to make of her comments and hoped they were not a catalyst for folk-hero status again. Enough of that experience went with the first shooting on the property, and any publicity at this point unnerved him that a new set of thrill-chasers might try to infringe upon his privacy. A couple of well-placed bullets scared them off before, but he worried that might not be enough.

Those worries proved harmless, as the next week remained quiet, routine-filled days at Hank's Heaven. His biggest worry now concerned the first winter of his new life.

Conrad's aversion to manual labor reared its ugly head through all the firewood ordered from Wal-Mart. With all the trees on the property, a few chopped down would only help the topography, but he followed advice from his brother voiced years ago: "If you want something bad enough, and you have the money for it, you ought to have it." Money was not a problem, so ordering firewood certainly made him happier than taking an axe to one of HIS trees.

The nights turned colder, and at times, Conrad's affinity for warm climates left him longing for the deep south again, but for some reason, those emotions became fewer and farther between with each passing day. Maybe the 20-pound weight gain since retirement caused him to embrace cooler temperatures.

Got my winter weight on.

The most difficult task concerned the cleaning of the fireplace and the flu up through the chimney top. The previous owners failed to clean that part of the cabin, and Conrad was paranoid about starting a fire without a complete aeration of the fireplace. Hours spent cleaning, blowing, and cleaning again resulted in the best condition the fireplace had been in since its construction in the early 1960s. He could sleep without paranoia, although the smoke detectors placed a strategic distance from the fireplace were double-checked and triple-checked and quadruple-checked. With all the energy spent getting to this point in life, Conrad did not want to die from a simple smoke inhalation. The project completed, Conrad presented the filthiest countenance sustained since his baseball playing days on all dirt fields.

He was an absolute mess, but felt good about it. Instead of showering at the A-frame, he cannonballed into the small pond and allowed the freshwater to wash the soot and ash from his blackened body. The coldness of the water aroused every pore, and he stayed only a brief time, fearing hypothermia.

Getting inside quickly, he turned the purchased heating unit on high and wrapped in a blanket next to the unit, embraced the warmth – towling off several times and then re-wrapping in the blanket. Having been here since May 9th, he realized this was his first swim – and truly wasn't a swim as much as a quick dousing and out. He vowed to swim the next summer when the water warmed – swim in at least two of the ponds – probably not the second pond (which still needed a name). He wondered how much the fireplace would be utilized, for the heating unit appeared perfect for the small cabin. He remembered stories of trailer fires and house fires and other structure fires started by overheated units, but the progress of man certainly made these new units safer, and relatively inexpensive. The firewood purchased was nearly as costly as his projections for several months of electricity, but utilizing both should keep the over price fairly cost-efficient.

Now dry, Conrad pondered the effect snow would have on Hank's Heaven. He'd only been here a couple of times in winter's snow. When he couldn't fish, he didn't see any reason to come as a boy. Now, he figured bad weather would be a sure-fire way to isolate, because only a fool would enter Hank's Heaven when snow was on the ground.

Of course, he'd known quite a few fools in his lifetime, and might be one himself. He hoped the electricity would not go out, but the fireplace would serve as light and heat should that come about. One thing he pondered was a lineman for the power company entering his property. These people didn't fall into the definition of trespassers, so he'd cross that bridge when necessary. Probably would depend on his mood at the time, and how the lineman handled himself or herself.

December 21st rolled around and winter began like most winters in this state: very cold overnight and morning and fairly warm in the afternoon. This state's weather historically was predictably unpredictable. He remembered the Christmas morning when it snowed and then the temperature that afternoon was in the low 70s.

They wonder why they have tornados here.

A new animal fed this morning: a bobcat. He'd heard the bobcat's growl in the distance a few times, but hadn't actually seen one. This morning, the bobcat dined at one bin while Pewie ate in his usual spot. Obvious to Conrad that the two animals knew and respected each other, but didn't give each other any mind; however, each gave the other plenty of room to negotiate. Pewie seemed to keep a closer eye on the bobcat than the bobcat kept on the skunk.

Suddenly, a male cardinal flew to one of the birdfeeders closest to the bobcat. A growl immediately sounded, and the cardinal answered with a screech louder than any Conrad recalled from the birds. The two hissed and screeched for some time, making their sounds between bites of food. The observer mused about the irony of the situation: a brilliant red cardinal and a heretofore docile wildcat showcasing their hatred for each other's species.

"I'm going to name you, Mr. Cardinal, Denny, and you, Mr. Wildcat, Joe Beasman. Now, try to get along, although I know it might take years for that to happen. Still, we have a rule here at Hank's Heaven – no fighting."

Neither took their eyes off the other. Conrad knew they heard him, but assumed no understanding...kind of like the overwhelming majority of cardinals and wildcats known in his

116

lifetime. He hoped that, in time, the two would realize Conrad could like both of them, and then realized the irony of that as well – people were always after him to pick sides. On his property, he picked his own side.

As suddenly as the male appeared, a female cardinal flew in and perched for food. At first, she seemed oblivious to the bobcat, but her next move showed she had been ignoring him. She swooped the adversary and pecked at the back of his neck, deftly flying away and then returning for more pecking. The cat let out a nasty growl, actually leaping, claws at maximum, at the flying female as she dove for another pecking.

"No, no, no...we don't fight here. If you fight, you have to move on. Conrad pulled his glock, thinking a warning shot might eliminate the territorialism, although he knew a gunshot might scare everyone into never coming back...and might send Pewie into a place no one wanted Pewie to be.

The female cardinal returned to the perch and continued feeding. The bobcat shot a quick look at the birds, growled a low Gallaraga-style noise, and meandered back to the woods.

Three beeps of a delivery truck horn signaled Conrad that Wal-Mart returned with his latest order. He bought twice as many provisions as conjectured for need, figuring as long as they weren't perishables, anything unused in the winter could be kept indefinitely anyway. The animals became busier as well, and he noticed them more and more taking food away from the bins and to wherever their nests, dens, and/or lairs resided. Amused by their looking at him seemingly waiting for him to look away, he believed they played a game with him, and he played along, looking away at the precise moment for the squirrels, raccoons, and birds to feel they "stole" the food and were successfully making their "getaway".

Whether or not the game existed in their minds, Conrad enjoyed passing the time playing it – even if the game was solitaire.

Big salt blocks were placed within a few feet of the A-frame, knowing how difficult winter could be on the deer, which were his favorite visitors other than Gallaraga. One thing of continued surprise was that no animal ever attacked another in his presence – all got along in animal harmony in Hank's Heaven. He surmised that changed when off the property – speculating that peace treaties existed between the various species in viewing the property as a no-combat zone – a true refuge.

However, when Gallaraga was present, deer weren't. Sanctuary only pertained so far – a little trepidation led to longer life sometimes. Conrad remained somewhat trepidatious about the big cat, but the fear aroused in the first encounter seemed to have morphed into a degree of mutual respect, and the two obviously accepted each other's existence. Conrad hadn't shot Gallaraga; Gallaraga hadn't eaten Conrad.

Status quo was a good thing; however, Conrad felt the relationship would probably come to a head at some point, perhaps this winter when most of the game became inaccessible to the predator. He mused that perhaps he should wear his nastiest cologne – perhaps that would ward off Gallaraga should he get thoughts of human flesh.

Provisions put away, Conrad realized he veered off schedule today. Not a problem. He answered to no one but himself, and winter probably needed a revised schedule anyway. It wasn't like he could fish for several hours each day – probably would rarely fish in the cold. Perhaps he would substitute writing for fishing and record for posterity what it was like to leave humanity behind – encourage others like him that this lifestyle suited the right personality.

Several book publishers contacted him after the first killing, hoping to land him to a contract for his memoirs. Irritated more than flattered, Conrad wondered where in Hades these people were when he tried to be an author years ago and fell flat on his laptop face.

He might write again, but the writing would be for himself and no one else; that way, he knew everyone who read it would like it...him.

Maybe he would write an animal-based story. He could write about how a cardinal and a wildcat became friends.

No...Tom Clancy quoted Mark Twain saying, "The difference between fiction and nonfiction is that fiction has to make sense."

A cardinal and a wildcat friends: nonfiction only, because no one would ever believe it.

Chapter 18...Dreaming of Christmas Past

Christmas Day caused a flood of memories both good and bad, but overall good. This marked the first Christmas ever at Hank's Heaven, but his grandparents were always major players in ensuring a merry Christmas during Conrad's youth. They always selected the perfect present for him. He remembered, as a youth, thinking they must have extra sensory perception in gift-giving – that it was almost like they knew exactly what he wanted. He'd always told his parents his ultimate gift, but his parents never gave the ultimate – always the grandparents.

It was almost like the parents told the grandparents and...

Duh!

Age illuminates reality and Conrad shook his head in realizing the simple answer to how the grandparents always knew. Memories of one particular Christmas came to mind. The only thing he'd wanted was a rod and reel. Fishing with cane poles proved effective for the youngster, but now he was growing and felt qualified to use a real reel. Seldom disappointed about material things in his lifetime, he remembered the stomach falling when going through the many things under the tree that particular Christmas morning. He feigned excitement over the Scrabble game and Etch-a-Sketch along with performing a great scene of acting over the new basketball. The ball wasn't the leather Wilson Jet requested; rather, it was a cheap rubberized genuine imitation basketball. He knew his parents didn't possess a great deal of money and he never wanted to appear ungrateful for their constant sacrifices, but still, he was a kid, and the ball wasn't leather and the rod and reel didn't exist.

That Christmas, as always, they traveled to the big city to attend the grandparents' celebration. A beer-basted turkey with all the trimmings highlighted the meal, and of course, the Grandmother's egg nog made the perfect after-dinner drink young and old. Speculation ran through the family when it would inevitably be discovered to be spiked, and while the mystery of "who spiked the punch bowl" never was actually solved, most of the family believed Grandmother was the culprit herself. She never denied the allegations.

Around the Christmas tree adorned with presents for everyone, young Conrad spied his. It appeared much different in shape than all the others, which looked like the traditional boxes of toys. His was long and not very wide. Could it be?

Christmas afternoon saw the traditional family football game among the adults, and games of hide-and-go-seek and chase among the children. Finally the time came to open presents. Grandfather served as master of ceremonies and chief toy-distributor, and always went in age order. Finally, Conrad's name was called and the young boy was sure there was a special gleam in his Grandfather's eye when giving this particular present.

Tearing open the Santa Claus face-laden paper, elation stayed elation at the present being the best present ever: a shiny Zebco 202. Conrad nearly cried but knew he couldn't – young boys did not cry in those days no matter what, lest several adults chime in, "I'll give you something to cry about" and/or incessantly tease the remainder of the day. However, emotion overcame him and a huge hug took the Grandfather by surprise.

"Dammit to hell, boy, it's just a rod and reel."

"It's my rod and reel and it's the best present ever. Thank you Grandfather; thank you Grandmother. She beamed as well, as nothing pleased her more than seeing an appreciative child. Perhaps that's why they bonded so well – Conrad always expressed appreciation at all things great and small. This was great.

Zebco rods and reels stayed mainstays for the next five decades – even the saltwater Zebco Eagle was used for the first years in Florida before the company quit making them and he switched to the saltwater-traditional open-faced reels. Six Zebco reels ranging from a 202 to the 404 to the 33 stood at attention in his reel rack at the cabin. Saltwater reels lined up behind but had not been used in any of the ponds.

Christmas lunch was a bit different, but instead of taking time to cook a large bird, Conrad simply fixed what he liked the best: a New York strip steak, baked potato, and green beans plus a Pepsi. He lit a special candle that once upon a time was his mother's. She left behind a large cache of special candles – blessed by the Catholic Church. To Conrad's knowledge, none of the candles were blessed by pedophiles. He winced at even thinking that, but also garnered a sense of amusement nonetheless. He begged forgiveness as he said grace, and believed God possessed a sense of humor.

No White Christmas. Partly sunny skies and fifty-degree temperatures made for a nice day – a day Conrad felt would test his resolve at isolation. Christmas represented family and there was no family representation alive, although the presence of all the relatives who had gone to the great beyond could be felt this day. Oh, an Uncle remained alive, but they suffered estrangement and no longer recognized each other's existence.

After lunch and the subsequent nap, Conrad walked down to the A-frame to inspect the food bins. A bit more expensive foods were placed in the bins to celebrate the day, and the menagerie turned out in full force. Even Pewie's presence failed to turn the others away, others that included the family of deer, some turkeys, squirrels, and Joe Beasman. Animals don't kill when there's plenty of other food around – they're not human and that's a good thing. If there's one thing reinforced during the summer, fall and early winter, it's that wildlife were superior to human beings.

Conrad preferred their company, thus the isolation reinforced.

The remainder of the day went idly by, with the animals taking turns at the bins without a negative moment. Even when Denny and his mate dined at the feeder above Joe Beasman, the three merely ignored each other – Conrad speculated it was their way of saying Merry Christmas to each other. With cardinals and wildcats, ignoring was probably for the best.

The music rotation included Buffett's *Carribean Christmas,* Elvis's *Blue Christmas*, Willie Nelson's *Pretty Paper and other Christmas Songs*, Bing Crosby's *White Christmas,* and John Denver's *Rocky Mountain Christmas*. His favorite Christmas song was Elvis's title song, and also loved the King's version of *I'll Be Home For Christmas*. The animals seemed oblivious to the sounds, but each tune brought a different holiday memory for Conrad – each memory a cherished one.

Music was a staple in his grandparents' home. After the presents were unwrapped and thank yous exchanged, Grandmother always demanded that Uncle Jack sing and play guitar. He always feigned reluctance, but how reluctant was he when his guitar was in the front seat of his car? At first, the family sang along to the familiar holiday tunes, but then Uncle Jack went solo on several. Then, whenever he would want to make "The Old Man", as he called his father, cry, he would sing the classic "Old Shep". When the lyrics came about the young man having to do what he had to do to the beloved dog, it never failed to bring the Grandfather to crocodile tears. We all watched for the tears during the main lyrics, and his eyes never disappointed.

"Dammit to hell, Jack, why do you always have to sing that damned song?"

Later, he would make his son sing it again...with the same result.

The music would continue for an hour or two, then the families would disperse to their individual homes. The long trip back to Conrad's hometown took all of twenty minutes, and inevitably, he would fall asleep in the back seat and wake up the next morning in his comfy bed. So many Christmases came and went with that most wonderful routine.

Conrad was thankful for his family and knew he wouldn't be isolated if they were still alive.

Back at the cabin for the evening, Conrad tended to a small blaze in the fireplace – his first attempt since cleaning the flu. Everything went well and the smell of fresh hickory filled the cabin with a familiar aroma, and all smoke ran up and out the chimney. Conrad was pleased with the success and looked forward to building larger fires as the winter grew colder. He fixed some green tea with a spoonful of sugar, a new nightly ritual coinciding with the cold. He added a secret ingredient, a shot of Knob Creek – for medicinal purposes only, of course.

Sitting back on the couch, Conrad reflected on the seven months at Hank's Heaven, the highs and lows, but mostly highs which greatly outweighed the lows. No second-guessing the decision to isolate came, and deep gratitude to all those who went before him entered his prayer to God to close out the day.

With the last sip of tea downed, Conrad readied for bed. He looked out the window. Gallaraga made his familiar turn and his familiar lie down.

"Goodnight, Gallaraga, thanks for the protection. I guess I won't see you in the morning, but will see you again tomorrow night."

Sleep among precious memories came easy.

Chapter 19...The Cat who came in from the Cold

Winter deepened over the next several weeks, and the first snowfall greeted Hank's

Heaven with God's purest blanket. Several inches fell, covering the grounds, tree limbs and

fencelines. Cold, as it must, accompanied the whitestuff, and the combination of snow,

freezing rain and temperatures in the single digits made provision delivery virtually impossible.

Conrad prepared for this event, stocking up in the preceding months with enough to get him

through a month or more. Prolonged snow and cold spells seldom happened in the state, but

Conrad convinced himself his first year could well provide an exception.

Sure enough, an early February overnight brought a record cold temperature below the

zero mark, but the combination space heater and fireplace left the cabin a cozy nest. As a

youngster and young adult, Conrad detested snow and cold, refusing his Mother's insistence at

going out to play. He wanted no part of it then, but now, not feeling trapped inside the

confines of the cabin, even though he essentially was, he basked in the beauty and grandeur

that this cleansing of the air and soil brought to his corner of the world. Perhaps the knowledge

of the true isolation the snow and ice brought to Hank's Heaven calmed him. Only an idiot

would venture through this to enter the property and anyone entering the property in this

weather deserved the fate.

Despite the ways of his youth, Conrad enjoyed brief trips outside in the snow and cold.

He sojourned to the food bins near the A-frame, as he covered them overnight to keep

moisture out, and each needed uncovering at the start of the day. On this day, he heard a

chorus of tiny mews coming from beneath the house and, turning to greet the noises, observed four little faces looking out from behind their mama's back. One of his few surprises rested with the fact that no cats had been around, and now there were at least five (he did the math/biology and realized there had to be six). The previous owners told tales of wandering cats at various locations on the property but, until this morning, no cat other than Gallaraga and Joe Beasman made appearances.

Well, Duh, there are obviously two reasons why the kitty cats haven't been here: Gallaraga and Joe Beasman!

Not sure the human fear level of the mama kitty, Conrad opened the bin that Beasman seemed to prefer and scooped a generous portion into the bowl attached to the side. Unattaching the bowl, he walked over to the house and placed the bowl a few feet from the kittens. He realized they were too young to feed, but mama kitty definitely needed this type of nourishment.

"Your name, madam, henceforth, is Mama Kitty. I am Conrad Nevitt and am the proprietor of Hank's Heaven. Since you are guests on my property, I will provide food and water and apparently a place to raise your young'uns. The only rule at Hank's Heaven is no fighting on the property. You can come and go as you please – no one owns anybody here at Hank's. The only expectations rest in enjoying this precious gift called life."

Mama Kitty turned in a protective move regarding her kittens, but he could tell she sensed no danger. Being cautious, she waited for Conrad to move back to the other bins, and when he was, in her cat mind, a correct distance away, she moved toward the bowl and began dining. She didn't look up for about ten bites, which signaled Conrad the level of hunger, then she looked up after every couple of bites to make sure no movement forthcoming toward her or her kittens.

Mama Kitty displayed a solid black coat with white paws and a touch of white under her chin, but her kittens exhibited a complete array of colors. One was tiger-striped, one was cream-colored, one was black and gray, while one resembled the mother so exactly that the kitten could play the Mama in an animal movie about her life.

The wonders of nature...wonder if there were multiple fathers. Damned tomcats – impregnate and then disappear.

Conrad knew some humans who operated the same way, shirking responsibilities and simply moving on to the next conquest. These kittens would probably never know their father, but, as Bud Bundy stated, "Knowing who your father is is not always what it's cracked up to be."

Before returning to the cabin, Conrad went inside the A-frame to make sure the pipes worked. The previous evening, he put the faucet on a slight drip to keep the pipes from freezing, but knew that wasn't always an effective method. Fortunately, in this case the drip paid the dividend. He turned on the space heater, hoping to remember the need to come back down at night and turn it off. Fire seemed to be constantly on his mind in cold weather and, while not that much in material possessions would be lost should the structure burn, the touch of history would be gone forever, regardless of whether or not rebuilding would occur. He kept family scrapbooks and a number of family heirlooms here, and hated the idea of them being destroyed. Sometimes he exhibited more sentimentalism than he ever thought possible. He surmised the dead remained loved, and the living remained detested.

Walking the cabin door, the familiar scene of burning wood caressed his nostrils and put him in a great mood. He had some leftover steak, so he put some canned sweet corn with the meat to serve as lunch. After lunch and naptime, the weather warmed to the low-twenties, but a check of the National Weather Service app on his cellphone told him the forecast was for another record-breaking cold during the overnight. Minus-12 degrees with a wind chill of -30 caused chagrin, as worry about the animals dominated his thoughts. He thought of Mama Kitty and the kittens, but did not worry about them. The space heater warmed the floorboards, so they could acquire some degree of warmth under the house, away from the wind. He decided not to go back to the A-frame and allow the space heater to run overnight. The need to keep the kittens and Mama Kitty warm overcame his fear of the heater overloading.

Winter and the ignorance of Daylight Savings Time caused darkness to fall earlier, and he noticed his schedule in winter changed to an earlier bedtime. While he adored college basketball on television, there were only select teams still followed: Western Kentucky University, University of Kentucky, University of Louisville, Duke, Florida and Florida State. He never felt wishy-washy about liking them all despite the rivalry existing between each team's fans, even though he had been criticized in his lifetime that he needed to choose sides. Western Kentucky was always the only choice, for his alma mater, despite many shortcomings, remained his alma mater and he loved it just as a smacked-around dog remained loyal to its owner. Conrad despised the animosity many fans vented toward fans of other schools and vice versa.

Why can't people simply enjoy their team's success and not worry about the other guys? Of course, most of these fanatics couldn't find the campus of their beloved institutions – never been on it, never stepped foot on a college campus, and their education level matched their

crassness.

Conrad realized his own snobbery at that – the hypocrisy displayed at level of education mattering. But, he postulated, it does make a difference if a person actually tried to better themselves by attending a post-secondary institution. He didn't care if it was the military, cosmetology school, trade school, or college – do something after high school to better oneself. Too many people lived on high school glory – rec department all-stars, he called them – and rooted hard for a school like they'd devoted their lives to that institution, when, in all reality, they knew nothing about the university other than its sports teams.

None of his teams were playing on this night, and even the history channel showed nothing of interest...serving up a boring round-table debate about the causes of the Civil War. He did enjoy the spirited debate between those who were adamant the war was about slavery and those who were equally adamant the war was about states' rights.

The answer was a resounding YES. Arguments are so much fun to watch when everyone's right and no wants to admit it.

After that part of the debate, Conrad turned off the television, checked the space heater, and went into the bedroom. The winter routine became such, but this night produced an alarming change. When he looked outside prior to the tap on the window, Gallaraga's absence came into view. There was no big cat between the cabin and the frozen pond – the first time since that first night's visit that the routine was broken.

Worry set in, but Conrad tried to quickly pass it off as a winter change. Gallaraga lived in a den on the northeast side, protected from the northeast wind. Conrad surmised it was simply too damned cold for the big cat to lie between the cabin and the frozen small pond, so there was no need to worry. He tossed and turned a bit more than usual, but finally fell asleep.

A weird noise woke the slumbering Conrad, one unheard since a family pet years ago made a similar noise. For a moment, his mind thought his beloved dog, Snowball, an eskimo spitz, was scratching to get into the bedroom. Coming to his senses, Conrad realized Snowball was long dead from a hit-and-run driver who never slowed down, and the scratching sounds were coming from the front door of the cabin. He was not in the first house he owned, he was in the last house he would own and someone wanted inside from the cold.

Knees popped loudly as the nearly 63 year-old man struggled to get out of bed, and they continued making breakfast cereal sounds as he maneuvered into the living room. Looking out the big picture window, the sight of the would-be entrant thrilled and frightened simultaneously.

Gallaraga scratched at the door again, this time emitting a low growl that seemed to say, "Hey dumbass, it's cold out here, let me in."

A myriad of thought processes brushed away all cobwebs. Conrad realized clarity of thought needed to be present before this decision was made. Does one allow such a predator into their home? Does it ruin their friendship to turn Gallaraga away? Why would he turn him away?

A line from one of his favorite *Star Trek: The Next Generation* characters came to mind. The Klingon Starfleet Officer Worf often quoted the Klingon axiom, "Today is a good day to die." The saying meant that, if the cause were just, dying was just as well, and to die doing an honorable thing produced the best death.

However, no one needed to die a foolish death, so Conrad picked up the glock and readied the weapon should the need arise. He hoped to show no fear, but that ship was sailing fast as his heart pounded faster than he could ever recall the pounding. Perhaps the last time he felt this way was batting leadoff in the American Baseball Congress championship game. Gallaraga would no doubt pickup on the heart rate and Conrad had no idea how that would play out. Still, the record-cold of the outside made the decision an easy one.

Opening the door with a great degree of slowness, almost to the point of the old *Inner Sanctum* radio play, Conrad stared into the eyes of the big cat. Gallaraga lifted a paw and smacked at the screen doorknob, enlightening the slightly shaking human that this was something that had happened before.

I wonder if Hank and Gallaraga enjoyed this kind of relationship, and he let the cat in to sit at the fireplace, too? Let's find out.

While fear exited, the grip on the glock did not, as Conrad opened the screen door, keeping the glock trained directly between the big cat's eyes. The cat seemed to understand, and lowered his body to crawl stealthily past the gun-wielding human. Gallaraga collapsed in front of the fire and moved to his side – a kitten-like maneuver whose body language says, "I'm not here to hurt anybody, I just want to relax and go to sleep."

Within moments, the feline fell asleep, panting and emitted a slight snore. There was little doubt this scene played out before with another person, so Uncle Hank and Gallaraga must have possessed at least a similar connection.

"Goodnight, Gallaraga, I'll see you in the morning, because somebody will have to let you out. Let me know when you want to go."

Conrad cautiously moved around the big cat, in between the feline and the fireplace. The caution was not out of fear of being attacked, but fear of waking up the sleeping beast. Sleep was needed by both, and Conrad simply wanted his friend to get what appeared to be much-needed rest.

His friend...there now was no doubt. He locked the door to the bedroom and slept as soundly as he had since moving in.

Chapter 20...He let the Cat Out of The Bag

A loud growl shook the cabin. Conrad sat upright, and now empathized with the millions of American soldiers awakened by Louis Gossett, Jr. –style drill sergeants. A quick glance at the cellphone showed 5:50 a.m., which told him the big cat woke 20 minutes prior to him each morning. Glock in hand, Conrad moved into the living room, knees popping with each step – not as loud as the growl, but close.

Gallaraga stood next to the front door awaiting its opening. Conrad smiled.

"Time to go out, Gallaraga? You know that's my name for you, right? OK, don't bite me and I won't shoot you and everything will be fine...do we understand each other?"

He knew Gallaraga didn't care and was probably thinking, *just open the damned door.*

Walking around the big cat, he held the gun a couple of feet away, hoping no lunging and bad scenes would ruin a good morning. Door opened, Gallaraga reached up with his massive paw and, to Conrad's amusement, opened the screen door himself. He bounded out and continued moving, despite the door smacking into him on the way out. After a few feet down the path, Gallaraga stopped, turned and raised his head with a growl that seemed to say thank you for the warm place to sleep.

"Come back any time, Gallaraga. Always a place by the fire on the cold nights."

The big cat moved deftly to his left and bounded into the small valley, then up the hillside toward the northeast corner – his corner of Hank's Heaven.

The remainder of winter saw a revised but equally satisfying routine:

- 5:50   wakeup growl

- 6:15   breakfast

- 7:00   check the food bins and either turn off, turn on, or leave alone the
space heater in the A-frame

- 7:30   online reading

- 9:00   writing

- 12:00   lunch

- 1:00   naptime

- 3:00   re-check of the food bins and check of the animal kingdom

- 4:00   Happy Hour

- 5:30   Dinner

- 6:15   television time

- 10:00   let Gallaraga inside followed by bedtime

The days passed quickly as he approached his 63rd birthday, which landed a couple of months prior to his first anniversary at Hank's Heaven. One of the few special days he continued to celebrate was his birthday, but more because of the good family memories the day brought to mind than any other reason. His Mom always made the day beyond special, and to not honor it would, in his mind, dishonor her. That would never happen.

On the birthday, certain things must happen: cherry pie and Frank Sinatra music. Rather than cake, Conrad preferred a birthday pie, and like his father and his father before him, the number one choice in pies was cherry. Throughout his youth and into his thirties, his Mom always baked a cherry pie for him, unless Kroger, Winn-Dixie or Foodland ran a buy-one/get-one free on cherry pies that week. Candles strategically placed in the crust, Frank Sinatra singing in the background, Conrad would be encouraged to make a wish and blow out the candles. This year, the pie was a BOGO from Wal-Mart, who ironically ran the special his birthday week. He wondered if his Mom haunted the Wal-Mart gods to make this happen.

In life, she was as persuasive a woman as he'd known.

With a thawing in the weather, Gallaraga resumed the nightly ritual of sleeping between the cabin and the small pond. So, on his birthday morning, Conrad woke at 6:15, made breakfast, and began the late winter routine. He strolled down to the bins, slushing a bit in the melted snow. Tiny tracks remained visible to and from the bins and the forest, and he'd learned each type of track from comparing the pictures of the tracks with pictures online. No new species arrived in winter; all but the blue heron were accounted for this season. Expected back in the fall, the blue heron would be checked for the scar.

Pewie, sporting a heavier coat, dined alone, as was off-winter normal. Conrad took it as an early sign of spring and return to normalcy. Today saw a different side of Pewie, as he startled Conrad by coming up beside the lounge chair to receive a pat on the head, given with some degree of trepidation. Relieved that his emotions didn't trigger a reaction in the skunk, Conrad continued the patting of the head, and did not jump out of his skin when Pewie climbed into his lap and went to sleep.

"Guess you wanted a place to nap after feeding, huh? Well, happy birthday to me."

Since he didn't want to debate the merits of changing routine with a creature that could leave a lasting impression with a flip of its tail, Conrad changed routine and napped with Pewie. The consolation of the schedule change was lost in the realization that, in less than a year, he successfully forged a bond with the creatures of Hank's Heaven. He wondered how far their loyalty went. He preferred their company to that of humans, and figured their loyalty surpassed any human's, but mused that it wouldn't take much to be more loyal than the most disloyal creatures on the face of the earth.

After about an hour, Pewie left Conrad's lap and made his way back to the forest. Meanwhile, Joe Beasman made his way to his favorite bin, giving Conrad a familiar yawn when hearing his name.

"Joe Beasman, this is a little early in the day for you, isn't it? Did the relaxed atmosphere Pewie and I created bring you out a bit early?"

The wildcat looked up and yawned again, showing off his fangs and letting the man in the lounge chair know all was right in the world.

"Do you want to come up in my lap, too? Hell, I can keep napping – I've got nothing to do."

Joe Beasman finished his meal, yawned a third time, and disappeared into the forest as quickly as he appeared. It was his way.

On schedule, as soon as the wildcat left, Denny and his mate flew onto the feeder. They appeared to dine more ravenously this day, and Conrad guessed with mating season nearing, the creatures were building up strength. Parenthood, human or critter, sapped more strength than any other endeavor. Perhaps the bird seed needed fortifying nutrients. The two birds remained longer than usual but flew away at the first sight of Mama Kitty, who, emerged from under the house to take her place at the same bin where Joe Beasman dined. The kittens poked their heads from under the house, but stayed in semi-hiding, probably at the behest of their Mama. Mama Kitty paid no mind to the cardinals, as the simple rule of nature Conrad postulated early on held true: as long as there is food, creatures won't hunt other creatures.

Man is the only animal that is cruel – the only animal who inflicts pain for pleasure; man is the only animal that blushes...or needs to.

Twain's commentary on humanity took over Conrad's thoughts for a few minutes as he pondered his place in Hank's Heaven. Part of him believed the Native American creed that no one truly owned anything, but he also believed in give and take, friendship for friendship, live and let live. He felt more connected here than at any time living in the "real" world, and felt the friends made were superior to the "fiends" made during his lifetime. There were a couple of wonderful humans, like Jeff and Boone, but overall, the one constant in the people who invaded his life was their user mentalities. Perhaps there were two constants, if one considered constantly being disappointed in human behavior part of the equation.

I love people...especially when they're not around.

His favorite scene from *Barfly* played in his head, and Mickey Rourke's portrayal of disappointment in the human race was spot-on. Charles Bukowski's writing, inappropriate to many and understandably so, nailed humanity on so many levels. Never a fan of Bukowski's operation of personal affairs, still, Conrad respected the raw realism Bukowski portrayed in the majority of his works. He never required or taught the writer in his classes, but from time to time a student project would feature the writer. Not oddly, never a female presenter.

Several weeks passed since Conrad visited The Big Lake, not one to trod through the snow for that distance. With most of the path clear except for some slushy places, he decided to walk over and take a few pictures of the water to document this time of year. The walk proved uneventful, but the view at the end proved breathtaking. The water, fresh from winter's thaw, appeared cleansed to a glistening blue-green. He didn't walk the dam for fear of falling, but stood at the top of the hill overlooking the water with the same wonder felt at six years of age.

Hank's Heaven proved heaven on earth existed.

Turning to begin the walk back, a patch of ice greeted his right foot and down he went. Adrenaline surged as Conrad feared injury, losing control as he plunged down the hillside, maintaining the path but procuring little other control. Images of serious injuries flashed through his mind as helplessness grew with each meter passed on the way down toward the barn. Finally, his body slid into a sideways position on the path, and stopped. He laid still for a moment, taking inventory of aches and pains, starting at his head and working his way down.

Convinced of no serious injury, slowly Conrad rolled to a patch of ground devoid of ice and snow, and slowly erected himself. He straightened, and felt a twinge in his lower back just above the posterior crack. No intense pain, but a noticeable twinge continued as he took his first couple of steps, then the twinge disappeared after twenty yards or so of movement.

Feelings of good fortune caused great relief, and the rush of adrenaline remained. Thinking back to his athletic days, he thought about those times when after a grueling evening of basketball, he would invariably, upon showering, discover scratches and bruises that went unnoticed during competition. He wondered if that would hold true that evening.

The walk back to the cabin continued, and the closer he became, the more discussion came about with his right knee. Unnoticed during the first steps, probably due to his predilection to the back twinge, this pain was real and intensifying. No stranger to knee problems in his athletic career, he felt blessed at never suffering a serious knee injury. The irony of hurting it at this point, and hurting it simply walking a path, was not lost on him. Conrad laughed at the folly, and recalled his most serious ankle injury – sustained stepping incorrectly off a curb near Western Kentucky University's campus.

Injuries are injuries – no matter how they occur. As he limped into the cabin, all the athletic training symposiums came to mind. The debate of applying hot or cold to the injured leg came forth. So many theories.

His answer was always the same: Yes.

Ice packs placed in the front of the freezer primarily for this purpose were gathered, and he placed one each on either side of his right knee. The knee elevated, Conrad searched for and found the remote on the couch, hoping to take his mind off the pain by watching some mindless programming.

Channel surfing like the typical male, he found a documentary on HBO featuring one of his favorite all-time athletes, Joe Namath. Suddenly, the knee didn't hurt quite so much as he watched and listened to the rundown of the many and various serious injuries and surgeries Namath endured during and after his playing career. He suffered his injuries before medical science learned how to fix things properly. Conrad hoped he didn't have to turn his knee over to medical science despite his confidence in knee repairmen.

Once the ice packs turned body temperature, Conrad plugged in the heating pad never far from the couch. He allowed it to heat to maximum level before applying the pad to his knee, and enjoyed the intense heat far more than the intense cold of the ice packs. His love of hot over cold caused worry about being able to endure winter at Hank's Heaven, but he was proud that winter was almost over and he actually enjoyed the time here. As the documentary turned to other aspects of Namath's life, Conrad's thoughts turned to the value of this place in winter. No one, to his or his monitor's knowledge, entered the grounds during this season. Not one single trespasser these three months proved the value of the season coupled with the publicity gained through the killings teamed with the isolated location of Hank's Heaven.

The knee felt immensely better, and Conrad removed the heating pad. He stood, apprehensive of a deep knee bend, but confident it was okay to raise the leg and bend the knee. Once that move was successfully performed, Conrad deemed it necessary to leave things alone until the evening, and then re-apply the cold and hot treatments before bed. He moved with only a small amount of pain to the kitchen, fixed some lunch, took his second nap of the day, and contemplated what to do with the rest of the day. The knee would continue to be nursed, so some free-lance writing would consume the afternoon hours.

After writing several chapters of a fiction piece, Conrad decided he needed a shower. Personal hygiene, despite his isolation, remained paramount to him, as a hot shower, sometimes more than one, stayed a part of his daily regimen. Body odor was a major bugaboo with him personally, and he never enjoyed the smell of unattended armpit. The preoccupation with personal hygiene was one he thought would go away in isolation, but he found himself just as preoccupied with smelling good now as he ever had. It was personal. He still used the same shower gel and scented shampoo as always, brushed his teeth with a mint toothpaste several times a day, trimmed his beard into a well-manicured Van Dyke, and applied the same cologne discovered late in life: Encounter.

He didn't want encounters, but he adored how he smelled using Encounter.

Conrad realized his humor was worsening with age.

The knee responded well to the treatment and the walk to the A-frame gave only slight pain. A little more careful than usual entering the walk-in shower, the hot water seemed even more welcome than usual. He let the water wash all over him, and as expected, felt a few additional pains as the water found those locations that needed particular attention. The most obvious pain centered on his left arm, which made sense as it was the arm he first used to brace his fall. The knee apparently injured when he bounced left to right. He spied a scratch running along his forearm for several inches, and knew some rubbing alcohol and antiseptic cream were forthcoming to ensure sterilizing the injury.

A bruise appeared on his left shoulder, which worried him some because there was no pain associated with it. He learned a long time ago that pain could be advantageous and that no pain could be a dangerous sign of serious injury. The shoulder was rotated so he knew full range of motion was present, but the bruise continued to concern him and he knew it needed daily monitoring.

After the shower, Conrad walked out of the A-frame, checking on Mama Kitty and kittens before returning to the cabin. All seemed fine, and he noticed Mama Kitty's dish empty. He filled it before leaving, and she shot him a look that radiated warmth – something he never felt from most of the cats he'd owned in his life. Maybe it was because she knew she wasn't owned, or maybe it was because most of his cats, like most of the people in his life, took him for granted.

Mama Kitty did not.

Back at the cabin, Conrad re-applied heat and cold to the right knee, fixed dinner, then sat back on the couch to watch some television. March Madness was underway – one of his favorite times of the year. All of his favorite teams made the NCAA Tournament, so he had quite a bit of vested rooting interest. Again, routine would be broken as he would stay up a bit later watching the roundball and making fun of announcers. Once upon a time, he was a huge Dickie V. fan, but one too many "Unbelievable" comments left him turning the sound off when Mr. Vitale did a game. He didn't worry about it for the tournament, for ESPN didn't carry the games. Still, there were over-rated announcers such as Bill Raftery, who obviously was a nice guy finishing first in his profession despite little contribution to the Xs and Os of the sport, with a trademark drivel of "jdlfjalfjdsfjfjfjfjjfjffj" to start a game.

What the hell was that?

At least there was solace in Billy Packer's retirement. Conrad remembered Packer for being the perfect foil for a great coach and commentator, Al McGuire, and when the two teamed with his personal favorite, Dick Enberg, it made for great sports coverage. But when Packer no longer had McGuire, he was no longer good. Every year during Packer's tenure, Conrad wrote both the Corrupt Broadcasting System (CBS) and the National Corrupt Athletic Association (NCAA) complaining about the broadcast team. Not once were his complaints acknowledged.

Now, his only complaints would be toward himself, because he controlled his existence. With that, he lodged a complaint: in all of the excitement of the day, the cherry pie had not been cut. So, Conrad walked with only a slight limp to the kitchen, where he got the pie out of the fridge and placed one candle in the middle. The ceremony honored his 63rd year, but moreover, honored nearly a year of isolation successfully lived. He made a wish before blowing out the light.

Please allow me another year as good or better as this one.

At 10:00, Conrad remembered to go into the bedroom and tap on the window, so Gallaraga could go to sleep. The Big Cat went through the usual motions, and Conrad went back to the living room to finish watching a Kentucky victory. Louisville and Kentucky both won their first-round games, but Western Kentucky fell victim to the National Corrupt Athletic Association's decision to seed them incorrectly, pairing them with a bad first-round matchup. An overtime loss proved they belonged, but would not advance.

He woke shortly after 2:00 a.m. and happily noticed no pain in his knee. Apparently, early treatment paid off. However, the left shoulder began to make its presence known, with soreness evident. Two ibuprofen and a gulp of Gatorade later, it was off to bed. He looked out the window at the slumbering Gallaraga, resting on the fresh hay put out each evening to warm the ground.

Conrad enjoyed doing little things for the creatures of Hank's Heaven, and felt from them the gratitude seldom felt from humans.

Another day finished...Lord, thank you for granting another day and help me to make this one a good one. But in all things, not my will but yours be done.

Sixty-three felt good. He ranked today one of the best in his history. Wondering how long bliss would last, his restfulness was interrupted by the bing of his laptop, signaling a message came in. He remembered a time when he would never put a bing on his laptop – in the old days, too many messages would foment too many bings. These days, so few came in he would forget to check if not for the occasional notification noise.

I'll get it in the morning.

Little did he realize the course that bing would sail.

Chapter 21...Blast from the Past

Upon waking at 6:15 a.m., Conrad's first thoughts were not of the computer. He looked outside to see the imprint in the hay where Gallaraga spent the night. Walking into the living room, he was reminded of the message by the blinking light on the laptop.

They waited all night – they can wait another few minutes – whomever they are.

Speculation centered on Tom Howlett once again asking for a one-on-one interview. Perhaps this would be the day Conrad would finally relent – probably not. The young reporter earned positive marks with persistence without going overboard and patience with Conrad's sarcasm, cynicism, and other –sms. Someday, maybe...but not today.

Bacon and eggs eaten, and animal feeding bins checked, he called up his e-mail. His only surprise was the lack of the surprise at the sender: Cousin Red Nevitt.

Red was Conrad's second cousin and his father's first. They called him Key West Red following his stint as a navy pilot in the Florida Keys. The stint covered nearly four years at the height of the Viet Nam Conflict, and the only reason Red wasn't sent to Southeast Asia was a colonel who loved athletics. At 6'5" and a solid basketball player, he led the base team to the championship among the armed forces teams, a source of great pride to a colonel – especially one bucking for promotion. When overseas assignment papers came in, the officer asked the pilot if he planned to play another season of basketball for the colonel's team. The answer came in the form of wanting to, but apparently Viet Nam was the destination.

The colonel tossed the papers into the wastebasket, saying, "I want another championship."

Key West Red seldom left the Keys, and never for very long, except for one lengthy trip to his home area to "find himself", as he put it. His epiphany from the trip was retirement was a good thing, and Conrad remembered thinking he wouldn't need to travel 1200 miles and spend a month camping at various outdoor venues simply to know retirement was a good thing. Conrad retired the first day possible...as did Red.

The cousins, at most points of their lives, enjoyed a mentor/mentee relationship. Red was a decade older and took Conrad under his wing at an early age. Red taught Conrad virtually everything he knew about the outdoors. The older cousin's philosophies fell on eager ears, and the younger cousin put him on a pedestal, never missing a chance to be part of his life. Red's influence on Conrad's youth and young adulthood was immense and positive, with seldom a decision made without consultation. In nearly every case, Conrad took his cousin's advice and, in nearly every case, the advice rang true. Even the move to Florida marked the highpoint in Red's influence, and their relationship grew by leaps and bounds over a 13-year period each time they were together. The zenith moment came one night when Red apprised Conrad he was his most trusted friend.

The younger cousin smiled at the revelation, then the smile turned to darkness.

As happens sometimes with even the best of friends, a money matter caused the friendship's demise. Key West Red worshipped money, while Conrad couldn't care less about it as long as he had bills paid and a few dollars in his pocket. It was the one issue on which they were polar opposites, and that opposition reared an ugly head.

The sad part in Conrad's mind was the fact that Red owned plenty of money. Smart investments at the height of the market made a marvelous portfolio. The older cousin talked about money almost as much as about fishing, and Conrad listened politely, although big business and big bucks were of little interest to him. Conrad put together a solid, conservative retirement package – one currently paying great dividends for his simple lifestyle. Still, like most people who talk about money constantly, there was never enough. Conversations more and more ended with Key West Red's signature phrase:

"How much is enough?"

Conrad's answer always caused eye-rolling. "Enough to have all my bills paid and ten dollars in my pocket."

One night, Key West Red summoned his younger cousin to Red's townhouse overlooking the Gulf of Mexico. The location provided Conrad with his second favorite place on earth. Castnetting and catching sharks comprised two of his favorite things to do, and Red's expertise in both brought added respect and admiration – a higher pedestal.

However, the older cousin wanted Conrad to invest in a major deal he was into – the opportunity to make a great deal of money in a short period of time. All it took was $150 grand and he would turn it into a million in a week. Conrad wanted more information, but Red refused, telling him the less he knew the better. He simply should trust his mentor on this one.

After a great deal of soul-searching, Conrad couldn't pull the trigger on the deal. He profusely apologized to Red and expected understanding that he wouldn't risk the majority of his savings on a deal for which little information was forthcoming and little input was allowed.

Red's profanity-laced tirade about respect and loyalty to one's elders left Conrad speechless.

"Listen to me, you ungrateful little sonofabitch, you will f------ do what I tell you to do and give me the f------ money in the next 48 hours. Do you f------ understand?"

The anger in his voice told Conrad saying no was the right thing to do. The last person to talk to him that way was a high school basketball coach. During his playing days for the verbally abusive coach, he thought his name was "God Dammit Nevitt!"

He didn't like it then, and as an adult, he wasn't going to take it now.

Without saying a word, Conrad walked out of the townhouse, Key West Red's continuing rant following him out the door.

They hadn't spoken since. Now, there was an e-mail. The subheading aroused his interest.

Re: Need a favor.

Wi-fi quickly called the e-mail to be read. Conrad scanned each word, and re-read to make sure he understood:

Dear Conrad,

I know we had a bad spot, but I'm in a jam and I have nowhere to turn. I'll make a long story short. I lost everything. I lost my money. I lost my wife, which means I lost her money. I lost the townhouse. I lost my boat. I've got nothing.

I know you might not have forgiven me for all the yelling I did that night, but you once told me you would always be there if I needed a favor, and I need one badly. I need a place to stay for a little while. I know you shoot people who come on your property, but I also know you made an exception with that little girl who shot her parents.

I won't stay long, but I need a place and I will be glad to tell you everything once I arrive. I need to know right away, because I have to get moving right away. I'm afraid I won't ever get to see the Keys again after I leave.

I am at the end of my rope, Conrad, and I need you. I've never said please to anyone before for anything, but I'm saying please right now. If I haven't heard from you in 48 hours, I'll know the answer is no and I won't bother you again. I gave you a great many things when you were growing up and I ask you for this one thing now.

Conrad decided on a third reading, and this time, he counted the number of personal pronouns. Way too many, and it didn't take an English professor to know there were too many, plus, it didn't take a psychology professor to figure out this person was, not only in trouble, but still as self-centered, narcissistic a human being as anyone anywhere.

Still, he was family, and playing the card of his contributions to Conrad's life gave him food for thought. No decision would be made this moment. This, like the financial decision, needed a bit of time. He wrote back:

Re: Response to your request for favor

Dear Red,

You've given me plenty to think about and you've given me only a short time to think about it. My best answer right now is to do my Cleavon Little imitation from Blazing Saddles.

"Give me 24 hours to come up with a brilliant plan for saving this town."

Seriously, you will receive my answer tomorrow morning, first thing – you will receive it on this timeline.

An interesting aspect of their communications arose. Key West Red used "I" countless times while Conrad never used "I", but derivatives of "You" dominated. His own epiphany revealed that the reason the cousins always got along was that it was always about Red – never about Conrad.

He was intrigued for tomorrow to find out what he decided to do.

Chapter 22...Family Reunion

Conrad thought the e-mail would cause a lost night's sleep, but no problems in snoozeville. When it came time to tap the window, he mused that the response to his cousin should be to come at night between 10 and five, with no warning regarding Gallaraga. While not knowing what Gallaraga would do faced with Key West Red, Conrad's belief centered on the big cat not being thrilled about an intruder. The night daydream imagined Red walking up the path to the cabin and being greeted with claws, roars, and pinned back ears. Red probably wasn't as fast as he was in his playing days, so perhaps a mercy killing would be the scene. Conrad wondered about Gallaraga's capabilities and insights. Would he recognize Key West Red as family? Would he sense Conrad's animosity toward the relative? Would he simply go back up the hill and leave family matters well enough alone?

At precisely 24 hours from sending the response saying an answer would come in 24 hours, Conrad sent the message:

Dear Cousin Red,

As you know, people trespassing onto this property get shot. However, you will not be considered a trespasser and you will not be shot unless you commit a shootable offense while here. You will not criticize the lifestyle and there will be no discussion of the money matter that caused your excommunication from my life, unless it directly relates to the dilemma you currently find yourself in. There is one demand: let me know your arrival time so the incendiary devices strategically planted around the property can be turned off. Blowing you up is not the plan. Have a safe trip, and while your presence here is unwanted, the good times outweigh the bad and my Father would want me to provide a temporary haven for family. *See you when you get here.*

Conrad hesitated a moment, then hit "Send".

Almost immediately, a bing sounded.

Dear Conrad,

I understand the feelings and I will do nothing to irritate. I need a place for a few days while I work through this problem. I will arrive tomorrow at noon, give or take thirty minutes. I hope we can mend fences and I hope none blow up – especially those around me.

No doubt Key West Red was anxious to be there – obviously, he was on some electronic device that gave instant notification so he could instantly reply. Conrad wondered if Red was already on the journey north, because he knew the plan was always to break up the Keys to hometown journey into two days. Thoughts about Red being on the run entered the speculation, and fueled thoughts concerning the rumors about the origins of Red's money. Bartenders didn't get rich bartending, but sometimes, connections made while bartending, especially in the Keys, brought forth riches...and dangerous situations.

Crab traps along Boca Chika Key were filled with quick-rich schemes gone awry.

The day was spent in speculation on Red's situation and on how Conrad wanted to welcome, or unwelcome him. While his e-mail assured his cousin no shooting would take place due to trespassing, shooting never was ruled out. The phrase "shootable offense" denoted a great deal of leeway, as interpretation was Conrad's to make. Something offensive such as

"Hello" could most certainly constitute a shootable offense, should Conrad decide to, as Picard would say, "Make it so." Key West Red needed to be on ultra-best behavior, and that would be an act never witnessed. One of the traits that endeared and enraged was Red's outspokenness. He could urinate off a human being in a heartbeat, and Conrad would stop that heartbeat should Red fall into his usual habit of provoking anger in a person.

Interesting how the qualities one once adored and respected in a person become the qualities one detests the most.

So it was with Key West Red.

As Conrad tried to make the day as routine as possible, one major change related to the animals. None came around to feed, which caused their benefactor to question why. Was something going on he didn't know about? Looking up the hillside, he spotted Joe Beasman in a tree, looking out over the gates. Beasman's ears perked from time to time, giving concern that perhaps something or someone was moving along the outer edge of the property. At first, Conrad dismissed the hypothesis as over-thinking on his part, but later in the day, Pewie was spotted moving up the hillside and away from his normal spot, and the turkeys did not come down from their usual spot on the northwest hillside.

To confirm suspicion, Conrad expanded his gate monitor's range to a radius of 100 feet. The white light blinked on and off, so Conrad stealthily moved to investigate that area, wearing moccasins to lighten noise made by his feet, and moving along a set of trees seemed designed by God to provide cover for Conrad to inspect this area.

About fifty feet from the white light monitor, Conrad spotted what looked to be one of those newfangled automatic setup tents. He had almost purchased one, but then asked himself why, when he owned two structures, a barn and an SUV. A tent was not needed. He couldn't tell if anyone was inside, but looking another fifty feet away he saw a black Isuzu. Red's favorite vehicle in his lifetime was a black Isuzu, but he hadn't owned one in several years, opting instead for sportier vehicles designed to impress the ladies. Conrad was never impressed by his choices, but Conrad was no lady.

The back of the tent was to Conrad, and he immediately thought that a stupid maneuver if the camper was indeed Red. No way Conrad would have his back to Hank's Heaven, given the violence toward intruders. Keep a site-line on the property was the smart thing to do, and no one thought of himself any smarter than Key West Red. That was another trait that, in the beginning, endeared him to Conrad but, in the end, infuriated the younger cousin. No matter what the debate, Key West Red was always right and Conrad was always wrong.

"I'm the genius in the family, remember that, young man. My IQ is off the charts and being smarter than everyone else serves me well."

As a young boy, Conrad believed that to be confidence and factual more than arrogant. It took a long time to realize it was more arrogance than factual. Having worked with high IQ-ed people all his life, Conrad maintained that the amount of IQ points negatively corresponded with common sense points, and those who thought themselves superior correspondingly underestimated their "inferiors". No doubt Red underestimated Conrad, and continued to do so.

Conrad knew himself capable of pulling the trigger on Key West Red, and was relatively sure his older cousin didn't believe that was possible. Conrad also realized one of his other thoughts came true: Red was already on the run when he sent the e-mail – no other explanation for him already being here. He wouldn't have flown in as he hadn't gotten into a plane since being shot down flying a reconnaissance maneuver near Cuba in the sixties. At least that was his story, and why Conrad never doubted it came into the younger cousin's mind for the first time.

Duh!

No debate on whether to let Red know his campsite was known. Conrad didn't care enough, and the good news was Red wouldn't be late for the noon appointment. Being early for appointments was one of the few things they still shared. The younger cousin simply stealthed away the same as he stealthed in, but would make sure to monitor the monitor more closely. Once back at the cabin, he placed his fitbit, a newfangled device on which he'd placed a multitude of fun and not-so-fun apps, on his wrist and pushed the app for "monitor the monitor". If someone, Red, entered the property at any point the remainder of the day or the next morning, the proper light would go off on the fitbit. He had planned to put it on in the morning anyway, but the early arrival put him on alert.

A late afternoon storm drove Conrad inside, and the thunder and lightning crashed and lit up the sky to the property owner's great amusement. The good Samaritan in him considered asking Key West Red onto the property and into the A-frame, but the fact that his older cousin was enduring some of nature's nastiest work amused Conrad greatly.

Let him get drenched and perhaps God will take care of my problem with one good bolt.

His biggest worry was the storm would knock the power out, as storms often did, and then the monitors would not function. In that case, he might simply shoot Key West Red for the general principal – blame him for the power going out, a shootable offense. However, as Conrad readied for bed, power remained on, and he worried little about his cousin entering the property. When Red wasn't working the bar, Conrad seldom saw him awake after 9:00, so didn't expect that to change this night. At 10:00, he tapped on the window, grateful the rain subsided, because Gallaraga didn't come down the hill on rainy nights. The big cat turned, but held his countenance a bit longer than usual toward Red's direction, almost as if he was letting Conrad know of Gallaraga's awareness concerning the situation.

The next morning brought a change in the big cat's routine, for he remained at the side of the cabin through breakfast. Conrad couldn't remember Gallaraga hanging around in the morning, but decided to bestow a reward and take some bacon out to him. Flipping the bacon strips in front of the surprise breakfast guest, Conrad was not surprised at how quickly the bacon became part of the cat's system. That familiar low growl followed and, instead of bounding up the hillside, Gallaraga went a different direction, bounding around to the back of the cabin.

Another first.

The routine morning passed on, and around 11:30 Conrad pressed the button on his control system, automatically opening both gates. It had been a while, but the green go light showed success in making the main path available to Red. The host didn't fret over the forthcoming conversation – he would listen and react accordingly.

Precisely at noon, the Isuzu made its way up the path to the cabin, with its lone occupant showing his age with a bit of a struggle to get out of the vehicle.

"It's hell to get old."

"In some cases, it beats the alternative. Sometimes not. It's like boxers or briefs: depends."

"I see your sense of humor hasn't changed with solitude."

"No, it remains a bad sense of humor but the great thing about isolation is I only have to amuse myself – and I'm easily amused."

"Well, Conrad, I'm happy to see you."

"Not sure I can say the same, but we'll see."

Key West Red looked around and inhaled deeply.

"I always loved this place. It's heaven on earth. I should have bought this place and you should have stayed in Florida."

"Two million dollars and it's yours."

"I used to say I've got problems, but money's not one of 'em. I can't say that today, and that's why I'm here. I need your help."

"Let's walk the grounds and you tell me your story."

"No hug for your Cousin Red?"

"No hug. Be happy. You are the first male on this property who wasn't shot on sight. So you are already ahead of the game. And that's what this probably is, but I'll listen and I will make no promises other than to listen and give you my best response, if a response is what you want."

"I need your best response, and I need for you to say you'll help me."

"We'll see...let's walk over to The Big Lake."

"I think that lake needs a name."

"It has its most appropriate name: The Big Lake. I figured Hank would like that, and I like it, so that's the name."

The cousins started the path toward the northwest corner of the property to view Key West Red's favorite spot of Hank's Heaven. He was old enough to remember watching it built, with Uncle Hank working his bulldozer like he had done it all his life; of course, he had operated a bulldozer his entire adult life.

As they walked along the path, Red appeared to put off the main conversation by trying to go down memory lane.

"Yeah, I remember Uncle Hank working his ass off building this place, but he didn't want to overbuild – wanted to keep as much of the property unspoiled as possible. Guess he was successful. Lots of good times here. I tell you, Conrad, The Big Lake is my favorite freshwater lake. You remember, I caught the state record bluegill in it that time we came up from the Keys."

Conrad remembered. They were in a canoe at an end of the lake seldom fished and Red yelled he had a big catfish on. He fought it for several minutes as it went deep, and finally managed to get it to the surface. Both fishermen were stunned to see a meat-platter-shaped bluegill nearly three times the size either had ever caught. They weighed the fish, took a picture, and put the beast of a panfish back in the water, later to find out it was a good six ounces more than the state record. Neither cared – it was all about the knowledge, not the trophy. Neither wanted to kill the magnificent fish, and that was mandatory to receive the recognition. Their fish story was true and that was all that mattered.

"I guess we should have taken him in and gotten the record, but I'm kinda glad we didn't. Hell, who knows? He might still be swimmin'."

"Doubtful. That fish would have to be fifty years old – don't think they live quite that long."

"Yes, but I let him live that day. Hope he lived out his days as happy ones. I think that's all anyone can ask – to live out their last days as happy ones."

"Okay, that's a great segue. Tell me what's going on."

"First, I want to take this in."

The two reached the top of the dam overlooking The Big Lake. Conrad felt Red's emotion at seeing it for the first time in many years – the pair fished this lake often in their youth and, for a moment, both transported to those carefree days of lots of fun with little responsibility.

"Been catching any of the big ones?"

"Summer and fall were fabulous in all three, but this one remains best. Biggest bass I caught was about six pounds with a bunch in the 2-5 pound range. Caught some big brim, but none like the record...plate size was the biggest. A few crappie here and there and got broken off by a few denizens of the deep. I think I might have hooked one of those big carp Uncle Hank always talked about."

"No catfish?"

"None in any of the three ponds. They have to be there. We stocked all three several times. Guess they went into the mud and don't come up. I've thought about putting out a trotline and see if that gets them, but I'll wind up getting turtles hooked and don't want that."

"We used to do that and get those turtles. Not many people like turtle any better than I do – you know that. We used to get the big ones and fix up some genuine burgoo – great stuff."

"Never acquired a taste for turtle. Like a good fish dinner from time to time, but something about eating a reptile turns me off."

The two men walked across the dam and sat down on the ancient bench by water's edge.

"O.K., tell me why you're here."

"Nice job of rigging these rodholders to the bench. Good job."

"Tell me why you're here."

"Can't I just enjoy the moment here?"

"The moment's up. Tell me why you're here. I won't ask again."

"Or what? Gonna pull out that glock and put one between my eyes? I've done nothing that's a, what did you call it, shootable offense?"

"If I ask you to do something and you don't do it…"

Key West Red realized the serious tone and that his former companion was not the same youngster he'd always known. Red knew how to manipulate Conrad, or at least, he used to know. He realized the need to comply with this man's rules.

Time to tell the sad tale.

Chapter 23...Confession is Good for the Soul

For the first time in all these years together, Conrad sensed nervousness as Key West Red began his story.

"Conrad, I'm in deep shit, to say the least. I don't have to remind you about how much I love money and I got a big opportunity to use my bar to make some. This one group of guys became regulars at the bar – I thought it was because they liked the bar and liked listening to me pontificate on things of the mind and the spirit. Well, that wasn't what they were doing. They were scoping out the joint to see if they could use it for their dealings. It all began with a couple of test runs, where they blatantly did deals in front of me – smalltime stuff that wouldn't be a big deal even if I turned them in.

One night, after they'd done this a few times, I told them I had a room in the back that I was thinking about turning into a V.I.P. room – that they could use it anytime for their business. They started doing that, and each night they did business, I'd find a bit of cash on the table – these guys were big tippers.

It stayed smalltime for a while, but then one night, they asked me if I was interested in getting more involved. I told them enthusiastically yes, and didn't even have to think. So, after the bar closed that night, we met in the back, and this new guy came in. I knew him from somewhere but couldn't remember where. I guess, as the old saying goes, he made me an offer about money I couldn't refuse – wanted me to use the bar to launder money going from Chicago to Madisonville to Nashville to Atlanta to Key West to Havana. Mine would be the next to last stop and would involve a shitload of cash money.

He was a helluva nice guy and said he had Western Kentucky ties, but didn't say anything else. Since I was a Western man, too, we hit it off talking about places like The Yellow Hydren, The College Inn, Horsebadorties and Mr. D's. By the end of the night, I could tell he wanted me to get in and to do well."

Conrad sat in silence, pretending to listen with the same respect he'd shown Red for 55 years or so. But it was an act, as he wasn't interested in the tale, until his attention perked at the Western Kentucky mention. His memory kicked in; however, he dismissed the possibility as too coincidental and too strange even for nonfiction. It was worth a question.

"So, did this guy have a name?"

"You sure you want to know?"

"Yeah, it will help separate him from the others. What do I care what he does?"

"His name is Arturo Palizzino."

Conrad's eyebrow raised Spock-like. Red failed to notice, too enthralled with himself over his storytelling abilities.

"The Palizzino family made solid inroads into the Miami to Cuba drug trafficking by moving a big portion of it to Key West. But they didn't have a dependable headquarters, and when they found my big back storeroom, they thought it perfect for the last segment before Havana."

"How many shipments did it take before you decided to take one for yourself, and just how stupid are you?"

Key West Red bristled at the remark, but completed the story.

"The first two went off without a hitch. We used faux beer delivery trucks and filled the 'kegs' with the money. They returned three days later filled with the 'product'. It was the third shipment of money when I got curious how much, and opened one of the kegs. Conrad, they weren't filled with five-dollar bills or ten-dollar bills – they were filled with 100-dollar bills and there were one time 50, one time 48, so I figured I could take two if the third shipment had 50 and no one would notice.

They noticed. Two members of the Palizzino family came in and told me two kegs were unaccounted, and the missing ones were my responsibility. I feigned ignorance, but they didn't care...said they'd be back in 24 hours to collect those kegs or the Key West crabs were about to get fatter.

So I got the hell out and came up here, figuring I could stash the money here and live out my days in whichever place you weren't living. I got enough cash money we can order anything we want, anytime we want. I don't know how much money you have, but you know our old saying: how much is enough? Bottom line, Conrad, I want to join you here. You owe me and I can't believe you, after all the socializing you did in your life, don't want someone, especially family, around. I can be a big help around here and you owe me big-time. You need to let me stay."

"All I need to do is stay white and die."

Conrad enjoyed the coldness of his delivery, and continued his frigid, nearly monotone monologue.

"You bring this down on me and expect me to just welcome you with open arms? Dammit to hell, Red, these people play for keeps and have enough firepower to blow this entire place to smithereens. You waltz in here like you own the place, after me telling you to never 'grace' my presence again, and expect me to just take you in and risk everything that's been built over the past year? What the hell you been smokin'?"

"They won't look here. I made sure of it. In my conversation with the Boss, Palizzino, when he asked me about any ties in this state, I told him I was related to The Trespasser Killer, but we'd fallen out and you told me you'd kill me if you ever saw me again. This would be the very last place they'd look for me. Conrad, I need to stay here even if I have to camp on The Big Lake. If you don't want me on this side, I can get supplies and build something over there. Tell me what I need to do to stay here."

"Give me 24 hours to think it over, like I did with the e-mail. I don't like acting impulsively, and after all, you're right – you are family. I hate seeing anyone as crab food and the family ghosts would probably haunt me forever if I said no; but I might say no, so be prepared to leave if I tell you. Tonight, you can stay in the A-frame and tomorrow I'll decide what to do. Now let's walk back; you've screwed up my schedule, you've made me miss my nap, and it's almost time for dinner."

"I think this was a little more important than a nap."

"Opinions vary."

The cousins walked back to the cabin, where Red vowed to move the Isuzu down the hill to the A-frame. Conrad wanted no sign of Red at the cabin in case Palizzino's men came calling. He watched Red go around to the driver's side door and a negative thought ran through Conrad's head. Before he could act on the thought, the fear came true. Coming around the side of the Isuzu, Red pointed a weapon straight at his cousin's heart.

"You always were too trusting of a soul – what a dumbass! I tried to give you an opportunity to get into this game, but I could read you were going to say no and then one of us would have to die. I would rather it be you than me."

Conrad stared at the weapon and grimaced.

"Yep, little cuz, it's a glock just like yours. I know how much you love irony, and I thought it a great idea that, if I had to kill you, I kill you with the weapon you've used to kill. Call it poetic justice."

Sadness filled Conrad for multiple reasons, but perhaps the saddest part of his about-to-die scenario was he could see no guilt in his older cousin. During his longtime friendship, people constantly told him Red embodied evil and could not be trusted. For years, the younger cousin staunchly defended the older, and now, in what appeared to be the final moments of their relationship, he had to admit they were right and he was wrong.

The scene altered abruptly. In a moment's notice, glock went flying through the air and Key West Red laid screaming under a mountain – a mountain named Gallaraga. The big cat must have been on the cabin roof the whole time and picked the ultimately appropriate moment to arbitrate the dispute. His right paw held Red's neck in place, while his body loomed a few inches above the would-be killer's. The cat seemed to be waiting for something, and Conrad realized he was waiting for his friend to take over.

Pulling his glock out of its holster, Conrad also realized Gallaraga believed the kill did not belong to the cat, but to the human.

"Thank you, Gallaraga, for this and many things. I can take it from here."

With understanding, the cat backed off, but not before swiping his right claws up and down Red's chest, making marks deep enough to ooze but not gush blood.

"My turn."

Two bullets rang forth, one for each leg. Conrad aimed well enough that the bullets passed through, leaving holes in each.

"Dammit to hell, Conrad, go ahead and finish me off you worthless old sonofabitch!"

Conrad bristled at being called old. Another bullet rang, this one passing through the right shoulder.

"Dammit! Dammit! Damn you! I'll see you in hell, Conrad Nevitt."

Several movie lines went through his head, such as Clint Eastwood's "Yeah" from *Unforgiven* or "You first" from several. He searched for an original line and wasn't sure at the authenticity, but liked the wordplay.

"I've used three bullets and that's a waste of two – not going to waste another right now. How much is enough? Apparently three bullets and one scratchmark at this point."

Gallaraga remained, which surprised Conrad, given three gunshots. He surmised the big cat wasn't leaving until his friend's safety was assured, to which that friend was eternally grateful. This scene officially marked the changing of the guard – best friend status switched from Key West Red to Gallaraga – the smartest change of his life.

"Are you just going to stand there like an idiot? Finish me, you bastard."

"If I planned to finish you, death would have already come with the first bullet, or I could have asked Gallaraga to do it – I believe he was most capable. No, I have a much better fate for you. For the moment, you can just lie there and bleed while I work out the details."

Picking up the other glock, he holstered the weapon which fit perfectly. Now with a hand free, he reached into his pocket for his phone. Selecting the phone app, he hit autodial from the last call made.

"Good afternoon, PST Trucking Company. How may I direct your call?"

"This is Conrad Nevitt. Mr. Palizzino is expecting my call."

Chapter 23...Returning the Favors

"Conrad, mi amigo, I appreciate you getting back with me so soon. Tell me some good news."

"First, tell me why you greeted me with Spanish!"

The longtime friends laughed at the two men, one Italian and the other Scotch-Irish, engaged in another language altogether.

"Ah, it's good in my business to know as many languages as possible."

"Hell, Arte, I'm still trying to master American."

"Oui. Me too. It's good to talk with you my friend, and I hope you bear good tidings. How is the family?"

"I'm with family right now, and we are having a holy conversation about things of the mind and the spirit. You know, Arte, family is hard to control sometimes, but I have certain members under complete control. I've caused them a great deal of pain just in the last couple of minutes, but I'm hoping to help eliminate their pain."

"Good friend, is there any way my company could be of service?"

"You know, now that you ask it, I need a package picked up as soon as possible. It's a heavy one, about 200 pounds. How much would your company charge for pickup?"

"After what you did for me in college, I told you, I owed you a favor. I will be glad to pickup the package and deliver it wherever you want."

"How about a delivery to, say, a Key West bar?"

"Hmm...that can be arranged. Now, would there be anything accompanying the package? Say, two kegs?

"Oh, I'll have to give that some additional thought. Hold that thought for just a moment while I walk past the package and look into a vehicle."

Conrad walked past the bleeding Red, busy tearing at his already ripped shirt to use pieces to plug the three holes. Looking inside, Conrad instantly spotted the two kegs in the back of the vehicle.

"Ah, Arte my friend, yes, I have the items in question and would be most happy to put them out, along with the larger package, in front of my cabin door. I will guarantee safe passage for your pickup and delivery men to come onto my property as welcome guests rather than trespassers."

"I definitely do not want them treated like trespassers – good pickup and delivery men are so hard to find these days, which is why I'm so interested in perhaps keeping your package for myself."

"By all means, monsieur, that will save me the cost of postage, will it not?"

"Agreed...and let me tell you that you can keep one of the two kegs for yourself – call it a bonus gift for all the good fellowship we've enjoyed through the years, or just call it a thank you for being the one person on the planet who knows how to keep his mouth shut about things that should not be talked about."

"While I am touched at your generous offer, Arte, I must respectfully decline. The entire set of packages belong to you, and all I ask is the ability to call upon you again should the situation ever arise that I need a favor."

"My word, sir, you have my word. As the Bible says, 'So let it be written; so let it be done.' My boys will arrive in the next three hours and will make sure they take everything you want them to take. They will be instructed that, if you have changed your mind, one of the kegs can stay."

"Again, the gesture is most appreciated, but I can't in good conscience accept it. Goes against my religion, or at least my own personal bro code. I'll look forward to getting rid of the packages and getting back to my serenity."

"We will communicate again soon, Conrad. Thanks for your help in this delivery matter."

"I am, and always shall be, yours."

"Live long and prosper."

Nothing else need to be said – Arturo Palizzino and Conrad Nevitt bonded in college the way few people did, with an incident nearly tragic. Both possessed solid memories.

A lovely Bowling Green spring day, and the two 19 year-olds, college sophomores, headed up the hill to Cherry Hall at the top of Western Kentucky University's campus. They always joked that it was all downhill after American Literature class, and that was more truth than fiction. On this particular day, Arte and Con took their usual seats in the middle of the class. Both knew professors tended to call on people at the front or the back, so the middle was THE place to be.

The chimes signaling the start of class rang but Professor Chestnut failed to appear. She was diligent about walking in at the precise end of the chimes, making a theatrical entrance grand enough that applause normally opened class. However, a graduate assistant strolled in, looking like he'd spent the previous night at the Yellow Hydren, and taking a piece of chalk, scribbled on the board:

NO CLASS TODAY. DR. CHESTNUT IS NOT FEELING WELL. NO ASSIGNMENTS. ENJOY.

Arte immediately stood and announced, "Party at Barren River Falls!"

Within an hour, the class re-convened at the small park overlooking what passed for falls on a Kentucky river. Food, beer and bourbon dominated the rest of the day as college youth partied like...well, college students. A great time had by all, until Arte decided to more closely examine the falls. Conrad, a veteran of such bodies of water, followed closely behind his Chicago-based friend, warning him to be careful.

The warning unheeded, sure enough, Arte slipped on a mossy rock, hitting his head on the way down to the water. Unsure as to the depth, Conrad cannonballed rather than dove to Arte, finding him right away, and struggling against the current and the Chicagoan's dead weight to pull them both to shore.

The fall left Arte unconscious. For the duration until paramedics arrived, Conrad held the cut head together, successfully stopping the flow of blood from the gash. There were numerous tense moments until they arrived at Bowling Green-Warren County Hospital. Time moved

slowly for the next several hours until Arte moved out of ICU into a regular room.

When he awoke, the first face seen was Conrad's.

"Scared us, man. Glad you're still with us."

"I need drugs. My head feels like it's split open."

"There's a logical reason for that. It was. They've got you all sewn up and you're going

to be fine – looks like a concussion so you'll stay here a few days, but you're all right."

"Last thing I remember is you telling me not to fall and then, dammit, I fell. Did you pull

me out?"

"Yeah, you would have done the same for me."

"Yes, I would have, but you did it. Listen, dude, I will always owe you, and my family

never forgets to repay favors."

Conrad continued to be amazed at the one person he could count on was considered a

top ten public enemy by most of the country – including the FBI.

Three and a half hours later, a black Hummer drove up the path to where Key West Red

laid in between two kegs of non-beer. Conrad watched from the picture window inside the

cabin, satisfied that the right path was chosen.

"Boys, listen, we can negotiate. I got problems, but money is not one of them. I can pay

you big money to let me go."

The scene played out like a pitiful final scene in a B movie, but something dawned on Conrad and he realized he needed to intervene. Walking out of the cabin, gun by his side, he approached the cleanup crew.

"A moment, gentlemen."

A look of relief passed through Red's countenance and he knew forgiveness was possible on both sides; after all, they were family. Red looked up at his captors with a look of *You're about to get yours.*

"Smugness and arrogance are not good colors on you, Cousin Red."

"Arturo said to be accommodating to you, Mr. Nevitt, so what can we do for you other than not taking Mr. Smug here back to the shop?"

A tense moment reined as the two apparent hit men wondered if gunplay was about to rear its ugly head. They knew of Conrad's abilities and each put a hand on their pistols. What happened next brought an understanding smile to three of the four faces.

"Relax boys, we just have one minor thing to figure out and then everybody can be on their way."

Arrogance turned back to fear on Red's face as Arturo's men heeded the words.

The larger and seemingly older of the two spoke.

"Yes, Mr. Nevitt? Re-think the money situation?"

"Oh, hell no...you keep the money – that belongs to your family, not mine – not belonging to my family is why we're here in the first place. No, we just have to figure out what to do with the Isuzu. If you want it, one of you can take it. If you don't want it, then I need you to do something important for me."

The two looked at each other, and for the first time, Conrad noticed physical and manneristic similarities between them.

I guess all hitmen look alike.

"I don't want it."

"Yeah, we got plenty of transportation and it would just be one more thing. Why don't you keep it?"

"Don't you need to call Arte and clear it with him."

The two smiled knowing glances at each other, and almost seemed to be mocking with their answer, like they knew something Conrad didn't.

"No, we feel we can make that decision, Mr. Nevitt. You keep it – call it our token of gratitude for something we know was a hard decision. Artebigbucks told us you'd always been intensely loyal to people – especially family – and he said this had to be difficult for you to turn him over."

Conrad looked down at Red and a wave of sad sentimentality engulfed him.

"Yeah...but people earn what they get in this life, boys. Unfortunately, Red earned what's happened. Uh...Artebigbucks? Does he know you call him that behind his back?"

"Hell, we call him that to his face – always have. Now, what favor do you need, Mr. Nevitt? We need to be on our way."

"Well, if you're going to leave the Isuzu here, I need the keys."

One of the hitmen reached into Red's pocket, produced the keys, and pitched them.

"Good doin' business with you, Mr. Nevitt. Drive it in peace."

"Thank you, boys. Tell Mr. Palizzino I send my best."

Key West Red re-entered the conversation.

"What the hell?! Conrad, Cousin, you can't let this happen. What would our parents say about you turning me over to these bastards? Change your mind, blow them away, and all will be forgiven. Hell, you can keep the Isuzu – no one will ever hear from me again. I'll go back to Florida and never be heard from again. C'mon, man, we've been through too much together to let it end like this."

Conrad shook his head that Key West Red continued to believe he could talk his way out of anything. It showed he didn't understand family, and thus didn't deserve to be in this one – or that one. After all, the two men sent to pick him up were brothers.

Both bore the last name Palizzino.

Chapter 24...The Calm after the Storm

After the Palizzino boys left, life returned to semi-normal for a few days. Conrad's routine returned and the animals with it; of course, they remained an integral part of the routine. Gallaraga returned to his sleep and wake habit, with one exception being to wait a few minutes longer to leave. The reason for the wait was because Conrad increased the amount of bacon prepared for the big cat. Then Gallaraga would bound across the dam and up the hillside like before, rather than the one-time bound to the back of the cabin in order to leap onto the roof and perch in wait for the near-death experience of Conrad.

He noticed even more comfortability in the other animals' attitudes toward him, with even the turkeys feeding near his feet. He learned their habits were a bit quirkier than the other animals. They preferred food scattered around the grounds haphazardly, so he complied. As their fear of him lessened, so did the distance from his lounge chair to the scattered food until he spread some in a circle around what was fast becoming his favorite non-water spot.

The number of turkeys visiting daily ranged from four to ten, with four consistently attending the feeding and the other six varying, giving Conrad knowledge that the turkey population was alive and well on Hank's Heaven. He marveled at himself being able to recognize individual birds from one another.

Not all birds look alike.

Conrad named them in a somewhat cliché way: Moe, Curly, Larry and Shemp. The four stooges ran around, pecking at the ground, pecking at the water bowls, and sometimes pecking at each other – which is where the comparison to the classic comedy group resonated. Their

178

quickness made him think about a basketball team he coached when he was a young, full-spirited ball of fire, where four small middle school boys pressed the opposition all over the court while he rotated one of three tall people on the team in and out to guard the basket in case the opposition broke the press. He had tried playing all his big people and realized early in the season they couldn't win that way – speed, basketball smarts, and aggressiveness comprised the success formula for that particular team. That group taught him more about coaching than he taught them about playing. Heart and desire trump size and potential. Nature on Hank's Heaven reinforced that idea – the best animals were those who possessed the heart and desire to survive.

The missing included Pewie and companion, obviously still spooked by all the human activity. Conrad surmised that was for the best, because Pewie, of all the animals, needed calm most. It was to everyone's benefit that Pewie always err on the side of caution. He would return when he was comfortable.

Joe Beasman made an appearance, which immediately scattered the four stooges and friends. They dined only a short time longer, apparently buying into the always err on the side of caution maxim. On this day, Denny and his mate flew to the feeder, seemingly as much to annoy Beasman as to feed. They only poked at the bird seed, but constantly let their song go at full blast, causing Beasman to growl at them each time the shrill pitch hit its apex.

Seeing the wildcat feeding reminded Conrad to check on Mama Kitty and her kittens under the house. The small ones were growing by leaps and bounds and, while hadn't been seen feeding on the Kit Kaboodles in the bin set aside for them, must be eating at night based on the amount gone. Hopefully, they would start wandering around and getting a feel for the property that all of them shared. Conrad might own Hank's Heaven on paper, but no animal recognized that, nor should they.

Hank's Heaven belonged to all of them.

With spring nearing its official start, Conrad oiled the reels, changed the lines on several, and cleaned his tackle boxes. This ritual energized him year after year, but this time, in his first full spring here, gave forth intense emotional feelings.

When he picked up the Zebco 33, those emotions overcame him and tears streamed. Conrad wondered if the tears were because of the overall feelings that these reels represented, or because this model in particular evoked a specific sadness.

I remember it was right after my thirteenth birthday. Mom and Dad asked if I wanted a party to celebrate being a teenager, and were met with a vociferous no. It was awkward enough being this age, I didn't want a great deal of fuss about it. Cherry pie, immediate family, that was enough and that was provided. The only person missing was the one person I wanted there: Red. I understood – Red was in basic training at a naval airbase in Texas.

Still, not having heard from him and seeing no card marked Texas, saddened me greatly. Red always came through but apparently not today. I would have thought this day, given his penchant for sentimentality and loyalty to family, would not go unnoticed.

I remember Grandfather coming up and smacking me on the back in a way only he could. "Dammit boy, you made it this far. Guess I have to payoff the Vegas boys 'cause I bet them you wouldn't make it to 13!" He laughed that contagious laugh that made everyone follow suit.

After my favorite dinner: hamburgers, French fries, green beans and cherry pie (with a Pepsi – Mom only allowed me to drink soda for dinner on special occasions – it was always milk, iced tea or watered-down Kool-Aid), the time came to open presents.

Two shirts from Mom: one blue and one yellow. She always gave two shirts and then, I always experienced a conundrum. When I would put one on the next day, whether it was blue or yellow, she would be convinced I hated the other shirt. I tried to trip her up later in life by wearing them both, one on top of the other. All that achieved was convincing her I hated the one worn underneath.

I expected fishing equipment from my grandparents. That was their go-to gift for me, but this year I had to mask my disappointment at getting a tool belt. Granted, it was full of tools, but even then, any manual labor I did was purely by mistake, and a tool belt constituted the world's worst gift for a 13 year-old.

Disappointment masked well, I thanked them profusely, worried I went overboard to a point they would know I detested the gift. Then, Grandmother smiled that knowing smile, and Grandfather laughed out loud.

I remember her words exactly.

"Con, the tool belt is what some people would call a gag gift – we knew it was the worst possible thing to get you. Your real present is outside on the garage!"

My feet never moved so fast and I nearly knocked Dad down getting to the door and down to the garage, which was about fifty feet from the house. Perched exactly ten feet above the driveway, hanging proudly, was a brand new basketball goal, backboard and net. On the ground directly below the net was a brand new Spalding RSS, leather ball. Greatest gift since the Zebco 202 and, at the moment, I thought it might be the greatest gift ever.

I remember picking up the ball and rolling it in my hands, overcome with joy. I shot a layup and made it. I backed up to five feet and swished the shot. It didn't bother me when I backed up and threw up a brick from fifteen feet. It would be the first of many bricks laid on this goal, but I didn't care.

Intense hugging ensued and no 13 year-old was ever more appreciative. But what I didn't realize was this would be the second-best present of the day.

"One more!" Mom exclaimed.

She handed me a small package and I paid little attention to the shape, knowing it paled in comparison with the goal and ball.

But the brand new Zebco 33 – the top of the line in fishing reels – gave my heart an even greater jolt. The card attached said, "Don't catch 'em all...leave some for our next trip. See you soon!"

Cousin Red.

Conrad's mind debated the reason for the tears, and realized the sadness concerned the demise of his cousin, not his part in it or any guilt associated with it. Red received what he deserved – the changes in him brought the downfall. Realizing people change for the worse as often as people change for the better, his sadness was for the negative change and not for the result of the change. The emotion for Red was pity, not empathy or sympathy.

Sympathy comes between shit and syphilis in the dictionary.

Trying to change his mood, Conrad picked up his laptop and walked back to the lounge chair. When he summoned *The Pine City Daily News*, he was relieved to see no one he knew had died; of course, he wondered how long it would take to process Key West Red's situation, or even if Arte killed him right away. Torture might have been the order of the day, making an example for others who might attempt to cross the Palizzinos. Arte adored making videos and perhaps a "How to torture a schmuck" might make it on the mafia circuit. It would probably end with the body in a Key West crabtrap and the head on a post somewhere on the beach.

The southernmost point has a point – he could place the head atop that marker.

The mouse clicked onto Tom Howlett's column, and the subject interested the reader. Howlett wrote a follow-up on Catherine Smith's progress after her acquittal on the charges of killing her parents. Conrad enjoyed the writing and felt a sense of pride that she was doing better than anyone expected. She was enrolled in an online program designed to get her through high school and had been taken in my people who had no blood-relation – a doctor and his wife who always wanted a daughter but had no children.

She fell into an outhouse and came out with a new suit of clothes.

Near the end of the story, Catherine reiterated her gratefulness to Conrad and said she hoped to repay his kindness. Worry about her making the mistake of returning was set aside when reading one of her last quotes, "...but he wants to be left alone, and the greatest gift we can all give him is to honor his wishes."

Good girl!

Placing the laptop to his side, Conrad decided to nap early. The events of the eleven months took somewhat of a toll and he found himself increasingly weary. He hoped his health was fine and realized, at 63, he wasn't 13 anymore. Snoozetime came easily.

He was awakened by a creature licking his hand, which had fallen over the side of the lounge chair. Looking down, Conrad smiled and welcomed Pewie back to their kind of civilization.

"Hey, Pewie, welcome back. Everything going well for you?"

The answer came when Pewie walked over to his favorite bin. Following were his companion and what looked like three exact replicas of Mother and Father skunk.

"Oh, you've been busy."

A nice thought entered Conrad's mind: Pewie's lack of fear would extend to his companion and children, so new friends were being made. Conrad looked forward to watching them grow, just as watching the kittens grow and all the other animals grow intrigued him.

Life was grand at Hank's Heaven as the one-year anniversary approached. As Conrad rose from the lounge chair, an air of uneasiness tugged at him. The feeling was difficult to pinpoint – was it continued worry about trespassers, apprehension about the fate of Key West

Red and Conrad's part in it, fear of personal illness, or something else altogether?

With May 9th approaching, he realized it was something else altogether.

Chapter 25...Little Red Riding Hoodlum

Everyone suffers through bad days – May 9th was the usual for Conrad. For some reason throughout his life, bad things happened on that date each year. He tried to change his fortune by moving into Hank's Heaven on May 9th – it worked...for one year.

On the morning of May 9th, Conrad planned to celebrate the first-year anniversary of isolation. He named it "Planned Serendipity Day" – loved the oxymoronic feel. Enjoying the animals, catching a few fish, eating his favorite foods, and listening to his finest music comprised a picture-book day, and planned serendipity.

The day was perfect...for a moment in time. A ding on his laptop during the middle of his breakfast was put aside until after Gallaraga got his bacon. However, once the e-mail opened, he knew the day was about to go downhill.

The message emanated from his second cousin, Rachel Nevitt-Roarke. The snooty side of the family, Rachel encompassed everything he despised in a human being, especially those of her gender. Her sense of entitlement was second to none; her sense of snobbery was second to none; her sense of arrogance was second to none; her sense of sense was behind virtually everyone in the free or un-free world.

Rachel Nevitt-Roarke was Key West Red's only child.

The message was the usual "flowery and then ask something" style of a young lady who had been coddled since birth. Red gave her everything she asked for, and she asked for everything she could think of. The best of everything was handed on a silver platter – unless she preferred gold – and what she gave in return was dismissiveness to everyone, a look down her nose to all she perceived to be subordinates...which included everyone, including her father. There was a time he tried to rein her in, but after failing several times, Red realized the damage had been done and she was too far pampered to do anything about. But instead of cutting her off and making her live on her own, he blamed himself and spoiled her even more. To say she was born with a silver spoon in her mouth was a gross understatement – a silver soup ladle was more like it, and she indulged in everything from jewels to men...the jewels were treated with far more humanity.

Conrad's relationship with Nevitt-Roarke was laissez-faire. While she was jealous of his closeness to her father, and often bitched about him treating Conrad like the son he wished he had, the two never experienced a cross word. She appeared to respect Conrad, which was unusual since she showed no respect for anyone or anything else, but perhaps the respect came due to his refusal to bend over backwards and do her bidding like everyone else. About the only thing they shared was a love of *Star Trek: The Next* Generation, and when their conversations recalled favorite episodes, they got along well. Otherwise, conversations were strained at best. He spoke directly to her and told her like it was, and she seemed to be okay with that. Most people felt sympathy for her losing her Mother early in life. She was two years old when Key West Red's wife was lost in a boating accident. Details were sketchy and Conrad wanted to buy the "she slipped and fell off the boat and drowned" story. The police bought it, but then again, they bought the same story about Natalie Wood.

Rachel married the lowest of low lifes – a guy who truly believed that when he left the bathroom, no aroma was left behind. Roarke and Rachel met at the craps tables in Atlantic

City, and their relationship was crap from the get-go. No love ever was present – other than their mutual love of gambling. They aspired to greater wealth, which they equated with superiority over people, and stayed together nearly a decade until the bottom fell out. Jet-setting lasted until it came time to pay the fiddler. He was an accountant who possessed no sense of accountability – another trait husband and wife shared about themselves. When she piled up personal gambling debts nearing seven figures, Roarke filed for divorce, and Rachel entered rehabilitation for drug, alcohol, gambling and depression.

Her call to Conrad about the end of her marriage signaled to him how bad off she was. The one person she turned to didn't like her. Out of loyalty to her father, Conrad helped. It was he who admitted her to the clinic, and he who talked her father into forgiving her trespasses. The two rekindled, and Conrad always felt good about his mediation in their decade-long disputes.

Now, he read the e-mail.

Dear Conrad,

I can't find my father. Do you have any clue where he is? No one has seen him for some time, and I'm tired of running the bar. The last thing I knew, he was in some kind of trouble. Did he turn to you for help? I don't know what he was into, but it must have been bad. You are the one person I think he would ask, because you are such a great man. My father and I love you. If you don't know where he is, would you help me find him? I will make it worth your time. Please e-mail back or text me. That's why my number is in the sub-heading. Please...I need to find him or at least know what happened to him. Thank you. Hugs and kisses.

Rachel

Conrad wanted to ignore the e-mail, and read it a second and third time. The one thing he was sure of concerned her statement that she didn't know what he was into. That was pure, unadulterated bullshit. Hemingway said, "Everyone should have a built-in shit detector." His went off big-time. He knew Rachel as one of the great liars of modern times.

The only way to tell Rachel Nevitt-Roarke was lying was if her lips were moving.

He picked up his cellphone, thought for a minute, then typed in her number for a text:

Rachel,

Tell me what you know and I'll tell you what little I know. Suffice it to say he contacted me, but I couldn't help him given the nature of the problem.

Immediately, he received a reply.

Conrad,

All I know is he was in over his head with some heavy dudes. He asked me to run the bar while he traveled to talk with you, and the night after he left, these guys came in – Italian mafia-type dudes. They tore up the backroom and shot a couple of our patrons. They held me down and wanted me to give them information on Daddy, but I didn't tell them a thing. They believed me – you know I'm a good actress so I fooled them into thinking I didn't know anything. I never told them about you. Help me. They said they were coming back and I better know something then.

Conrad smiled and shook his head. The only thing he believed about the text was that she was good actress, but even that wasn't true – she was a great actress. Always had been.

189

She was playing him for information. It made him glad he contacted Arte – she probably sold them all out and, if he hadn't told Arte what was going on, he might have had hell to pay. He started to ask why she hadn't warned him, but he already knew the answer.

They got him, Rachel. He came here and they knew where he was headed. It was almost like they knew he was here before he knew he was coming.

The phone rang after his text.

"You don't think I turned him in, do you? You know me better than that. I would never rat out my father. I am insulted."

"My guess it's not the first time. No, I don't think you turned him in, because he would have been caught before he got here."

"Did they kill him in front of you?"

"No, just took him away."

"Hmm…oh, did they take the Isuzu?"

Conrad realized what this was all about. She was worried about the car, and probably wanted it back. Another thought went through his head, and if he knew her as well as he believed, he knew her next step.

"No, they gave it to me with instructions to shut the hell up, so I shut the hell up. Probably shouldn't be telling you what I've told you."

"I'm coming to get my car."

"That would be a bad idea."

"You wouldn't shoot me, would you, cousin?"

"Don't bet your life on it. Besides, how would you get here and get it back to the Keys?"

"You let me worry about that. I'll be there tomorrow and get the car. It belongs to me – it's the last thing I have of my Daddy's besides this damned bar."

"Alright, Rachel, I'll let you come and get it…one free pass for old time's sake."

"Thank you, cousin, you always were my favorite. Oh, by the way, you haven't looked in the Isuzu, have you? I have a couple of things in it that I need."

"Naw, it's just been sitting here. I haven't driven it at all or even been in it. I'll be glad to get it off my property. For all I know, it has drug money it, but the boys who hauled him away didn't seem to want the vehicle."

"Oh, good…well, I want my things and the car means so much to me. Thank you, cousin, for letting me do this."

"How are you going to get here so quickly?" he re-questioned.

"Don't worry – you know me, I have my ways of getting things done."

"Yes, you always did. Let's hope your luck continues."

"It will. I've had a bad run lately, so you know my old saying on the craps table: shoot to get hot, shoot to stay hot."

"That's gotten you into trouble more than once."

"I've always been able to get out ahead of the game."

"Charmed life."

"Always."

When Conrad pushed "End" on the phone, he wondered how long her luck would hold. He remembered the classic Daryl Royal quote: "Luck is when preparation meets opportunity."

Conrad decided to be prepared.

Chapter 26...The Fairytale Ends in a Grim(m) Way

The remainder of his first anniversary in Hank's Heaven followed a more familiar routine. The dogwood in bloom meant the crappie were biting everything in sight before their spawn. It was the only time of year Conrad used the artificial lure "li'l skunk", a small fly-like invention that his Grandfather loved to use year-round. Conrad fished all three ponds and caught crappie and small bass in all three. Although several of the crappie were definite keepers, each was carefully released to be caught again at some point.

After lunch and the afternoon nap, the bing summoned him to open his laptop again.

Conrad,

I've got a question for you: do you have a place big enough for a helicopter to land? The gentleman I'm seeing now offered his helicopter for my trip, but it won't do me any good if I can't land it there.

XOXO

After thinking for a moment and realizing what was really going on, Conrad responded.

Rachel,

There's a nice big field adjacent to the A-frame. If your pilot navigates the trees around it okay, then it should make a decent landing pad. Feel free to use it.

Live long and prosper.

Moments later, she gave the proper Vulcan-style response.

Peace and long life. See you tomorrow.

While Conrad would not be surprised at Rachel's ability to manipulate a man into loaning his helicopter, he realized there was more to the story. Knowing her penchant for lying when the truth was better, Conrad believed she owned a helicopter – further proving a theory that would be validated in 24 hours. If he was wrong, it was no big deal. But erring the other way could be fatal when dealing with someone of Rachel's personality.

The next morning, during the bacon feeding, Conrad knelt by Gallaraga's side and patted the beast's neck. The big cat immediately raised his head, beckoning his friend to scratch under his neck – his favorite place for scratching. Hoping Gallaraga would understand, Conrad issued a warning.

"Big Guy, when you leave today, take your usual route. Don't go up on the roof. It's not going to be safe around here, and I don't want anything happening to you."

Conrad pointed to the dam and the hillside.

"Do your usual thing and get out of here until tonight. Go up there and, hopefully, we'll get back in our routine tonight."

He moved behind the cat and, when Gallaraga finished the bacon and stood up to leave, Conrad once again pointed to the dam and hillside. The big cat seemed somewhat reluctant, almost knowing danger was in the air, but honored his friend's wishes by bounding across the dam and up the hillside. This day, however, he stopped just past the bench on the other side of the small pond (which still needed a name) and let out one of the loudest growls heard on the property. Conrad felt it was a "I'll be around if you need me" message.

He hoped his plan worked and nothing else would be needed.

The full complement of animals dined at the bins, and Conrad and his laptop sat in their midst, but instead of calling up the internet, he spoke directly to them all.

"You all want to be scarce today. Eat hearty, my friends, because I'm not 100 percent sure I'll be around to feed you after today. An evil presence is coming – a human we can't trust…yeah, I know, an untrustworthy human is an ultimate oxymoron. Thanks for the look, Joe Beasman. Listen, if I don't make it through the day, you all keep getting along. Don't eat each other – eat other things to survive – things you don't know. I know you don't understand anything I'm saying, but it helps me to say them out loud. I've sent my last will and testament to Mr. Goldstein, and this land will become part of the nature preserve next door, so everybody should remain safe and the money I leave should help keep everybody fed so you don't have to eat each other. Even though, Beasman, I know if you ever get ahold of Denny, he's a dead bird – can't say as I blame you for that with all the taunting he's given you.

That's about it. I love all of you guys and hope to survive today, but you all need to get the hell out of Dodge today. I'll be back down in a little while and, if you're still here, I'll run off everybody but Mama Kitty and the kittens. They should be okay under the house. So long, my friends, be well."

With his speech finished, and the comprehension by the animals seeming equal to that of a composition II class listening to a lecture about how to write a literary criticism paper, he trudged up the path to the cabin. As he walked in, the monitor light of the main gate blinked. Were they early? He hit the communications button.

"Are you guys early?"

"What guys? I can't believe you're expecting anyone – that sure ain't like you."

"Who the hell is this?"

"Mr. Nevitt, it's Catherine."

"Catherine, you need to go away...now! I can't tell you why, but some feces is going down on this property today and you need to not be here. Go away!"

"Can't I help? You know I'm pretty good with a gun."

"Yes, Catherine, I know that, but I also know that your gun is under safekeeping in my bedroom drawer."

"Can I have it back? I might need to shoot someone again."

"Bad idea, Miss Smith...please, go. Tell you what, come back in a couple of days and I will let you in."

"Promise?"

"You have my word that you will not be considered a trespasser. Now go before my guests arrive."

"Mr. Nevitt, you be careful and I'll see you soon."

"O.K. Good day, Catherine."

He breathed a sigh of relief, averting the crisis of someone he actually liked getting involved in what was bound to be a bloody day. He thanked God and then, as always when he thought of God, said his favorite prayer:

God, grant me the serenity to accept the things I cannot change...the courage to change the things I can...and the wisdom to know the difference.

Feeling better as always after recitation, he loaded his rifle, double-checked his glock and, for reasons unknown to him other than paranoia and over-preparedness, walked into the bedroom and opened the dresser drawer. He took out Catherine's pistol, remembering there were two empty chambers. Reloading the gun, he then placed it back in the drawer.

One can never have enough firepower on days like today.

The owner of Hank's Heaven fixed an early lunch – a gourmet peanut, butter and jelly sandwich, some potato chips and, on this day, a switch from Pepsi to Mountain Dew. The Dew had always been his favorite soda, but as he aged, the sugar boost it provided became unwanted, and he went from a six-Dew-a-day habit to only drinking one when extra energy demanded.

Today was such a day.

Around noon, glock in holster and rifle in hand, Conrad stepped out of the cabin and walked a few feet in order to check the roof. Relieved that the shadows on the roof were not Gallaraga's, he turned back toward the main gate and sat in the rocking chair strategically placed for this day.

The waiting game began, but the wait was not long.

A few minutes later, Conrad heard the sound of a whirligig coming over the trees. He watched it sway a bit in the wind as it slowly lowered into the field between the A-frame and the main gate. No animals could be seen, as they obviously heeded the warning. Mama Kitty was no doubt herding her kittens into the middle of the area beneath the house. Never have to worry about those types of cats – they take care of themselves well. Conrad, for the most part, identified with that. Sometimes he was probably overcautious – he was about to find out if today's precautions were justified.

Landing gently, the helicopter blades slowed rhythmically until they came to a complete stop. The one thing Conrad knew at that moment was the pilot knew what he was doing. Everything about the entry onto Hank's Heaven was perfect, and it lent to the hypothesis that the pilot did this often.

A small man with military-style buzzcut stepped out first, followed by Rachel, who was followed by a second man who looked a clone of the first. The two men dressed in black, and appeared steroid-laden, although Conrad surmised they sported vests that made them look larger than life. Each carried a rifle and each carried what appeared to be a holstered long knife at their respective sides. Rachel, on first glance appeared to be unarmed, but her appearance never jived with who she really was, so Conrad assumed somewhere on her body was at least one weapon.

Conrad remained seated, but his adrenaline flow increased with each step of Rachel and the Rachettes. Hopeful but knowing himself unprepared to go arm-to-arm with professional mercenaries, and wondering if professional mercenary was a department of redundancy department, Conrad worried the next moments would be his last. Thoughts raced through his brain like a computer overload, with facets from the lovely times of the past year to his childhood to Key West Red to anything and everything all in a minute.

When Rachel and the Rachettes moved to within about twenty feet of the rocking chair, Conrad put his hand up.

"Far enough, gentlemen. Rachel, I would say it's good to see you, but I'm not going to lie to you. We've said and heard enough lies in our lifetimes."

"Speak for yourself, Con."

"O.K., you've said enough lies and I've heard enough lies in our lifetimes...better?"

"Asshole."

"Thank you...now, here are the keys to the Isuzu. Take it and go."

"Do I smell a bit of fear in you, cousin?"

"I'm sure you do – these guys make me nervous, but I'm not surprised to see them. You never did anything without men around."

No response forthcoming as Rachel was more concerned with her Father's vehicle. She took the keys and, instead of getting in the driver's side to drive off, she opened the back. Immediate displeasure crossed her face and she shot a true Rachel look in Conrad's direction.

"Where in the hell are the kegs?"

"Kegs?"

"Don't play stupid, Conrad Nevitt, I don't play the stupid game. Daddy took two kegs with him when he left the bar, and they are mine. Now tell me where they are or else!"

"I don't have them, Rach, and never did. Does the name Arturo Palizzino mean anything to you?"

Her face paled.

"Don't tell me you're in cahoots with that murdering bastard! Lowlife scum is the best thing I can say about that sonofabitch. He blamed Daddy for a lost shipment and he couldn't have been more wrong."

"Because you took the shipment, not Cousin Red…and then he knew he was about to be killed for it, so he grabbed a couple of others and ran like a bat out of hell. I'll be you took a shipment to pay off gambling debts – debts to the Palizzino family in Atlantic City is my guess. You got into deep shit at the craps table for the umpteenth time and, for the umpteenth time, your Dad tried to bail your ass out. Dammit to hell, Rachel, how could you do that to your own father? But stop me if I'm wrong."

"Well, since you're either going to tell me where the money is or die anyway, I guess it's okay to tell you that, for the most part, you're right. But it was the roulette wheel and blackjack table, and the house was cheating. I only cheated right back and took the money that should have been mine anyway."

"Hard to believe...but I bet you get to the point where you lie so much you believe yourself. I've known you all your life, Rachel, and you've never taken personal responsibility for anything. It's always been someone else's fault. It was your parents or your teachers or your boss and now it's the casino. I would say grow up, little bitch, but that ship has sailed and fallen over the horizon."

"I'm only going to ask you one more time where the kegs are. Where are my kegs?"

"First of all, they were never your kegs, and second of all, I do know where they are. Your Dad brought them here, but then tried to kill me and take over my property – obviously, that didn't happen. I was going to give him the benefit of the doubt, but knew I'd better cover my ass just in case. There's something about me none of you – not one person in my family – knew about me, yet it's one of the most important things about me."

Rachel rolled her eyes in the dismissive way he'd seen many times from her, but he knew her curiosity was aroused.

"Okay, before I have you shot, tell me what we don't know about you, little piss-ant college professor."

"Arte Palizzino is one of my best friends – my best friend from college days on. Whenever I wanted money to fund a project the college wouldn't fund, all I had to do was make a phone call. We talked a couple of times a week and, while we didn't see each other much over the years, built a friendship like no other. I would die for him and he would die for me – it's that kind of bond. I turned your Dad's ass in to Arte because blood is not thicker than water when the water is wonderful and the blood is tainted – like your blood."

"Glad the little professor got his one last chance to lecture, and I listened probably better than any of those preppie bastards ever did. Any last words before I have you killed?"

"Yes...remember our great *Star Trek: The Next Generation* discussions?"

"They were definitely the only times I liked you. So what?"

"I want to play the 'Do you remember the episode where' game we played as kids...play it one last time."

She seemed amused, while her henchmen seemed antsy. Still, she was in charge and the discussion point was intriguing to her. The Trekker in her couldn't resist.

"Probably the most unusual last request of all time, but go for it."

"Do you remember the episode where the Romulan defector, thinking he was doing the right thing, came onto the Enterprise to warn Captain Picard about a Romulan military base near the neutral zone?"

"Yes, 'The Defector', one of my favorites. It showed doing the right thing can get you killed, which is what happened to the Romulan. What of it?"

"Well, first of all, that wasn't Roddenberry's point, but you would never understand giving one's life for a just cause having never understood just causes. But, do you remember what happened when the Enterprise went across the neutral zone to inspect the planet?"

"Of course, they didn't find anything and then Picard ordered Riker to take the ship out of harm's way, but the Romulan trap worked perfectly and they surrounded the ship. Stupid on the Enterprise's part."

"You need to go one more step in your memory bank."

"I – I don't recall what happened next."

"Just when the arrogant Romulan commander was bragging about destroying the Enterprise and displaying its hulk in the capital city, Picard raised his hand and, lo and behold, Klingon Birds of Prey appeared to even the odds."

"What are you saying?"

Conrad raised his hand and, on the roof of the cabin, on either side of the chimney, the Palizzino brothers appeared, rifle scopes trained on the Rachettes. Little red lights blazed on the foreheads of each man.

Just as in the science-fiction episode, the tables turned, and Conrad felt the need to do his best Patrick Stewart imitation, with an accent every bit as bad as Kevin Costner's British speech in *Robin Hood: Prince of Thieves*.

"What shall it be, Rachel? Shall we have a shootout and all die together. As our friend Worf said, 'Today is a good day to die'."

"You are no Jean Luc-Picard."

"No, as much as I hate to admit it, I'm more James Tiberius Kirk. Picard was a better man – he would never shoot unless it was a last resort. Kirk, he'd fire the photon torpedoes at the first opportunity. He believed in preserving the Enterprise at all costs, while Picard believed there was a time to chance losing it. I'm more Kirk, and that's why I'm about to do what I'm about to do."

"And what's that?"

Conrad lowered his hand and pointed toward the Rachettes.

"Make it so!"

Two shots rang out, dropping Rachel's protectors to the ground. In a flash, Conrad pulled his glock and fired a bullet through her shoulder, precisely the spot where he'd administered a shot to her Father.

"Damn you! Damn you! Damn you all to hell!" Rachel fell back and landed between her deceased would-be soldiers.

Conrad turned to the Palizzinos with a look of thanks, and their large smiles told him they were pleased to be a part. The brothers exchanged high fives and disappeared to the ladder at the back of the cabin.

Meanwhile, oblivious to the movement from Rachel, Conrad turned to see a small handgun pointed directly at him.

"Today is indeed a good day to die," coldly came from Rachel's mouth.

A gunblast followed, and Conrad braced for impact. He felt nothing and opened his eyes, expecting to see blood spurting from somewhere on his own body. Instead, he saw Rachel grasping her own bloody hand where a bullet pierced through. Around the side of the cabin appeared a young girl with a satisfied grin.

"We're even, Mr. Nevitt. Thanks for telling me where my gun was."

In his year of isolation, Conrad Nevitt was never so happy to see another human being.

"May I keep my gun?"

"Certainly, Catherine...I don't know what to say."

"Live long and prosper."

Chapter 27...Cleanup

After assuring the Palizzino brothers that Catherine was on their side, the foursome debated what to do with the remaining live enemy. It dawned on Conrad that the pilot remained unaccounted.

"Do we need to whack the pilot?"

The brothers smiled that knowing countenance that let their friend know he really wasn't ahead of the game.

"You mean Jimbo? Nah, he's Arte's favorite pilot. You're not the only person who keeps Arte in the loop when someone is trying to pull a fast one. This girl here used to sleep with Jimbo on a regular basis, and thought he ran his own outfit, which he does to a certain extent – but the outfit he runs answers to you-know-who."

"I should have known. I'm never ahead the The Man. That's why he's the Boss."

"Exactly."

Catherine remained quiet for most of the conversation, but chimed in at this point.

"Are you going to kill her? Can I do it?"

She immediately saw disappointment in Conrad's face and backed off the conversation.

"What do you think we ought to do with you, Rachel?"

"You bastards can go to hell. I want to see Arte."

"Your wish is our command. Boys, I'll bet Arte would love to see her – maybe re-unite her with other beloved family members, eh?"

"I think you're right, Mr. Nevitt. C'mon, Miss Priss, let's give you a nice ride back. You don't mind if we take your rental helicopter, do you? Oh, that's right, it's our helicopter, so we don't have to ask your permission."

The brothers lifted her to her feet, with one applying a bandage to her bleeding shoulder, not wanting her to bleed on his jogging suit.

"Hey guys, can you hold her up right here in front of me for a moment? I have something for her."

They turned her to face directly in front of Conrad, who immediately took out his glock and fired a bullet into each leg.

"Just wanted you to match Key West Red. Like father, like daughter. I know how Arte likes consistency."

Everyone laughed but one, who was too busy hurting and bleeding to find the humor in the moment.

"What about the little girl?"

"She'll be fine. I'll take it from here boys. You deal with the big girl and I'll deal with the younger one."

Conrad thought for a moment, then retracted.

"Wait a minute, gentlemen, let me find out something and maybe we can work out something in everybody's best interest. Catherine, you said you needed to ask me something. Is it what I think it is? Do you need a place to stay?"

"Yes, Mr. Nevitt. I'm just not happy in the foster home – all they want to do is cash the check for me. It's not that they treat me bad, it's that they don't treat me at all. I need somebody who will care for me and make me get things done. All they want is the money. I want to live here."

"Well, that's not going to happen, but I know for a fact someone who is looking for a daughter and he might just be willing to take a chance on you. If you want someone to hold your butt to the fire, he and his wife are the perfect couple to do that."

One of the brothers picked up on the train of thought.

"Hell, yes, Conrad. I think you've got something. No doubt Arte and the Mrs. would be thrilled and we wouldn't have to worry about any paperwork."

"What do you say, Catherine, want me to find out if the most powerful man in the country would want you as a daughter?"

"Shit! Shit! Oh my god, shit! Yes…"

"Don't get your hopes up, yet, let me make a call."

Speed dial and transfer accomplished, the deal was made.

"O.K., hey boys, you got room on that chopper for one more?"

"Yeah, 'cause I'm gonna need to take the Isuzu to get these bodies to the waste management center. You don't mind, do you?"

"I never claimed the car as mine – consider it yours. You'll find the keys on Rachel over there. Dammit to hell, Rachel, you've got blood on them. I could just kill you."

Again, Rachel failed to see the humor and launched a spate of color metaphors Conrad's way.

"C'mon, Catherine, help me load this trash into the copter. Ever flown before?"

"No sir."

While one brother loaded the bodies into the Isuzu, the other walked the still-bleeding Rachel to the copter, but smartly handcuffing her before starting the walk. Catherine assisted like a pro, and the two bonded quickly.

"So can I call you Uncle?"

"Sure, and my name is Vincente. My friends call me Vinnie."

"O.K., Uncle Vinnie."

Conrad seemed the only one to get the inside joke, but that was okay – it wasn't the first time in his life he found obscure humor.

Before stepping into the whirligig, Catherine ran to Conrad and gave him a bear hug.

"Thanks for caring?"

"I always will...and I need to ask you one favor."

"Anything."

"Don't ever come back. I'm tired and I want to be alone. E-mail, text, keep in touch, but don't ever come back. Someone always gets shot when you're around!"

Smiles exchanged, Catherine entered the copter, which Jimbo expertly guided back into the sky and away. Moments later, Bocaccio, the other brother, drove by, waving goodbye.

"So long, Uncle Buck!"

Conrad shook his head at another movie reference.

Back at the cabin, Conrad noticed the main gate light flickering on and off, and it showed it had been on since shortly after the helicopter's arrival. That explained how Catherine got on the property. She must have waited for him to be distracted, and the copter certainly provided that, and snuck onto the property, sneaking around the back hillside and into the back of the cabin. There she procured the gun from the bedroom dresser and proceeded to save his life. He wasn't sure how she got by the soon-to-be Uncle Vinnie and Uncle Buck, but young girls have their ways. He wasn't questioning – he was grateful.

The cellphone sounded, and he looked at the number.

"Hey Arte, everybody's gone."

"Tell me more about Catherine. Angelina wants to know more. I haven't seen her this excited in a long time."

As Conrad, on speaker phone with Arte and Angelina, started recounting all he knew about Catherine Smith, Angelina would often interrupt, saying she knew that. Turned out, she'd wanted to adopt Catherine from the get-go and provide her with a home like no other could provide. Conrad didn't care what their line of business was, these two were a loving couple who would provide a loving atmosphere for Catherine – but proper discipline, missing from her life, would be instituted fairly and lovingly. The situation would not mirror the Key West Red/Rachel Nevitt-Roarke give her anything she wants scenario – the Palizzinos would provide the optimum growth environment for a teenage girl.

He was confident the young lady would embrace the tough love with all her heart.

While the major part of him was thrilled to simply be alive and equally thrilled at the positive turn of events, another part of him was truly urinated.

Dammit to hell...I missed my nap.

Chapter 28...Captain Conrad Catches the Great White Whale...er, Catfish

While part of him didn't care, Conrad often thought of his cousin Red and second cousin Rachel over the next few days, wondering about their fate. He scanned several websites each day specifically looking for a story or perhaps a clue or two about whatever Arte decided to do to the father/daughter thieves. As nice a guy as his friend was 90 percent of the time, there was that 10 percent where he was not only one of the most powerful men on the planet, but one who truly believed in punishing those who broke the code. In all the years of knowing Arte, Conrad never came close to breaking the code. His father trained him well to understand what dire consequences could mean, and he applied that understanding whenever dealing with Arte. Great guy – powerful guy – but he lived the honorable criminal code to a fault.

Honorable criminal was a great oxymoron.

Life continued peacefully on Hank's Heaven. Back in the routine, Conrad woke from his afternoon nap and decided to walk over to The Big Lake. He took his Zebco 33 and Zebco 404 along with the gate monitor, tackle box, and glock. Easing the canoe into the water, Conrad appreciated still being in good health; actually, after the events of the past couple of months, he appreciated being alive. These afternoons on the water, hopefully, would become more commonplace as spring begat summer. Drifting across the lake, he attached a purple artificial nightcrawler to the swivel on the end of the Zebco 33 line, and put a live nightcrawler on the hook attached to the swivel on the end of the Zebco 404 line. The live bait was trolled behind the canoe, while he worked the banks with the artificial nightcrawler.

Disappointed that the first twenty-five casts garnered nary a hit, cast twenty-six hit the jackpot. Feeling a huge tug, Conrad set the hook perfectly, nearly flipping himself in the canoe but balancing in the nick of time. The huge creature of the lake sped toward the middle and the fisherman was a bit amazed that any fish could pull the canoe with him in it. The canoe was lightweight indeed but it still took a helluva fish to be doing this. He kept the pressure on as the drag continued to sing intermittently between him gaining line and losing line. As was the case with him in freshwater or saltwater, all he wanted was the see the creature and revel in its majestic movements.

By the feel of things, this is a trophy bass.

Thoughts of whether or not to mount the fish on his wall were quickly dispersed when realizing the chances of landing the fish were not good. Someone forgot the landing net and there was no doubt who that was. More time passed and Conrad noticed the peculiarity of a bass staying so deep. By now, any other bass in the lake would have leaped out of the water several times. This fish stayed down and tried to manhandle the Zebco 33. Conrad congratulated himself on putting heavier line this year and using a heavier sinker – both of those changes from the norm gave him a better chance of landing the fish.

As the battle continued, he allowed his mind to wander to great fishing stories read, always transporting to pages of *The Old Man and the Sea*. Santiago fought the marlin page after page after page, and Conrad hoped his battle would not take the 86 pages or so that it took The Great Hemingway. While part of him was relieved that whatever creature this was would not be eaten by sharks, another part of him missed the thrill of shark fishing – his favorite type. He also scoffed at the idea of the fish on his line representing any Judeo-Christian theological figure – it was a fish, albeit a lunker.

Several minutes later, he felt the fish come off the bottom and realized the canoe was virtually dead-center in the lake. Conrad pulled hard straight up, caring and not caring whether the line broke or not, but ecstatic when he realized the line was holding and shortly he would see what should be the largest bass in the lake.

Breaking the surface was one of the pleasantest surprises of Conrad's fishing experience at Hank's Heaven.

If it's a bass, it grew whiskers during the battle.

The largest catfish Conrad ever hooked laid on its side next to the canoe. It was at least half the length of the canoe and about as wide. He realized that bringing it in the canoe was not an option, and that the only option would be to paddle the canoe to the shore, dragging the fish along. Looking at the channel catfish reminded him of *Grumpy Old Men* and their quest to land the legendary creature of the lake: Catfish Hunter. When they finally caught him, sentimentality got the best of them and Catfish Hunter was released to continue the legend. Conrad was not going to do that; at least, not without getting a picture first. The cellphone camera captured the catfish, with the canoe included for perspective, and then the decision needed to be made.

Of course, I could always just shoot the damned thing.

After laughing at his own remark, Conrad reached into his tacklebox for one of his favorite tools. He then brought what he believed to be the grand imperial poobah of The Big Lake closer to him. The fish, exhausted, switched from one side to the other, reminding Conrad of how he tossed and turned some nights.

"Mr. Moby Catfish, you are obviously the chief denizen of the deep waters of The Big Lake. I am your judge, jury, and executioner; however, I hereby grant you your freedom to continue to rule the bass, bluegill, crappie, turtles, otter, eel, and whatever other creatures invade your space in this, The Big Lake. Thank you for the battle, and please do not hold it against me for sticking a hook in your mouth. These hooks dissolve over time, so hopefully you won't suffer much discomfort. Again, thank you Mr. Moby, you can return to the depths."

With that, Conrad cut the line just above the swivel. He used his paddle to gently prod Moby for several minutes, as the catfish seemed to give up. It gasped for air and laid on one side, so Conrad would guide the paddle under him and move him upright, then move the paddle behind the dorsal fin on Moby's back and push forward, forcing him to take water into his tired gills.

Finally and rather suddenly, Moby Catfish sprung to life and created a spectacular splash, spraying water in all directions, including a drenching of Conrad. Moby skimmed across the top of the water for a few feet, then returned to the depths of The Big Lake.

Conrad breathed a sigh of relief. Moby Catfish deserved to roam these waters as he seemed as old as the lake itself. Looking up, Conrad thanked Uncle Hank and his Grandfather for the work put into Hank's Heaven, and hoped they approved of his actions today.

Some things deserve life.

No encore needed, Conrad paddled the canoe to the shore, pulled it out of the water and turned in over so rainwater would not cause problems. He thanked the Creator, said *The Serenity Prayer* again, and headed back to the cabin, pleased with himself for a successful day on the water.

No fish for dinner seemed the appropriate non-choice. Hot dogs, sauerkraut and baked beans highlighted the dinner menu. A couple of times, Conrad re-visited the photo of Moby, and each time basked in the delightful battle between the two that, today, Conrad won the battle, Moby won the war, and all won excitement. Today was a memory etched forever between human and catfish, and at least one of them was the better for it. So few catfish are caught on artificial nightcrawlers – Conrad bet one would never fool Moby again.

After dinner, he watched a struggling HooRays team on television – they weren't doing well but they were still his team and a long season remained. Conrad called up Yahoo News and sat back to scroll down for the latest news and sports of the day. Moments later, he shot back up to the edge of the couch as one of the most gruesome photos ever shown on Yahoo came into view.

Two rotting, human heads on stakes were driven into the marker at the southernmost point of the United States in Key West, Florida. A note attached to the marker served to warn others who would break any honor code among humanity.

Conrad now knew the fate of his cousins.

Some things deserve death.

Chapter 29...Brotherly Hate

For the next three months, life returned to wonderful routine. Spring turned into summer and, aside from a few deviations from the schedule, each day passed with the same joyful nature. No one disturbed him and he disturbed no one. The animals moved about at will on Hank's Heaven, and his learning curve continued to grow. Fishing continued to be bass/bluegill/crappie runs, with not a single catfish added to the catch. No signs of Moby, which was good news, for if the struggle between the Old Man and the Lake against Moby Catfish resulted in the fish's demise, he would have gone belly-up by now. Conrad checked every day, happy to not see a carcass, and knowing no bird of prey, even the largest ones, could succeed in carrying that big body away from the water.

The long summer nights did not seem so long. Baseball on DirectTV dominated the evening schedule, and his beloved HooRays surged to a better season once May and June became July and August. The formula of solid starting pitching and a great bullpen offset the fact that Conrad was 63 and felt he possessed a better chance of hitting than most of the team. Still, he enjoyed the games.

Daily Yahoo News checks showed no solid updates on the father/daughter murders that rocked the Keys, although occasionally a story ran that there was no story to tell. Arte occasionally updated on Catherine's progress toward full-fledged teenagerhood, and Conrad's heart warmed with each positive message. The Palizzinos obviously fell in love with the young lady, and she obviously was doing all the things she was supposed to do to remain a thriving member of the family.

An early August afternoon disrupted the reverie.

Conrad knew something was amiss when nary an animal was at the bins. While he had so much more to learn and knew he couldn't learn it in the time left, one thing he knew is that, when they weren't on their routines, something negative was in the air. Sure enough, Conrad's laptop monitor started flashing that someone was at the main gate. He activated the intercom.

"Who goes there?"

"Open the damned gate and don't shoot me. I'm coming in and I don't need your bullshit. Now, open the damned gate in the next couple of minutes or I'm going to take my big-ass vehicle through the f------ thing! Got that, boy?"

"Who is this, and who the hell do you think you are?"

"Conrad Nevitt, it's Uncle Harry, now open the damned gate. I'm 90 years old today and time's a wastin'. Do you understand me, boy?"

"Hang on, Harry, I'll open the gate, but I make no promises about not shooting your dumbass. You need to change the tone in your voice and you need to understand this property has nothing to do with you anymore. You are entering my home and will treat me accordingly. I'll give you a chance to give me a reason not to shoot you, but understand if you don't give me a good reason not to, you'll be dead on your birthday. Now, do you understand ME, old man?"

"Yeah, I understand, but you've got one minute to open this f------ gate, or you'll have to replace it."

Conrad activated the gate opener.

Uncle Harry's claim to fame was being that one relative every family seems to have –
the one no one wants to ever associate with, but no one ever wants to say that to his face.
Pompous, bombastic, mean-spirited only scratched the surface of descriptors Conrad heard
over the years. He was Conrad's great-uncle by marriage, so thankfully, no blood-relation. He
had one other claim to fame that was the only respect Conrad gave.

Harry was Uncle Hank's brother.

Remembering the few times he was around Harry, not one positive memory existed.
Conrad thought of the conversations his Grandfather would have with Hank every Sunday for
years before they would head to Heaven. Grandfather would ask if Harry was going to be
there; if the answer was yes, they didn't go. Conrad's Grandfather liked everybody – he
detested Harry. As the family story went, Harry made a pass at Grandmother one afternoon at
Hank's Heaven, and a fight resulted. Not many details were forthcoming, but the story
indicated Harry spent some degree of time at St. Francis Hospital. After that, they never went
to Hank's Heaven if Harry was going to be around.

Conrad's contact with Harry was minimal. All he knew was he didn't like Harry, either,
striking Conrad as someone who would argue the sky was really not blue and punctuating his
remarks with constant put-downs of his adversary. Being young, Conrad showed respect to his
elder, as he had been taught, always saying a polite "Yes, sir" or "No, sir", but he also knew
from family discussions that the only way to earn Harry's respect was to treat him as nastily as
he treated others. That was why Conrad's spiel let his great uncle (no blood relation) know

shooting was a distinct possibility. Any sign of weakness would be pounced upon, and the owner of Hank's Heaven figured shooting might be too good for this ornery old man.

He walked back to the cabin to wait for Harry and didn't wait long. A rickety, raggedy pickup truck that looked like it should have never left the farm coughed and sputtered up the path, stopping where the Isuzu once parked. Conrad, sitting in his rocking chair, glock in hand, was glad he didn't stand up when a streak of brownish gray flew by him and leaped with full fury onto the hood of the truck. Even when attacking Key West Red, Gallaraga never showed this type of pure primitive anger. No one needed to quality for a Rhodes Scholarship to realize Gallaraga wanted to kill Harry.

The driver of the truck did not seem surprised and, to Conrad's amazement, did not seem shaken. He simply reached under his seat and shot through the windshield, barely missing the beyond-angry feline. Gallaraga jumped off the hood and moved behind Conrad's rocking chair, still snarling at an alarming rate. Conrad stood up and got between the truck and the cat, realizing as he looked that Gallaraga might be out of control. Still, he knew some control had to take place or an ugly scene was about to take place.

"Gallaraga, I don't like the sonofabitch either, but I'm going to find out why he's here. You get up the hillside and let me handle it."

Whether the cat understood the words didn't matter as much as he understood the hand gesture toward the dam and hillside. Grudgingly obliging, nostrils flaring and heart beating in fierce palpitations, Gallaraga raced across the dam and up the hill.

"God------ varmints! Why Hank didn't kill that litter and eliminate the problem I don't know. Too damned nice for his own good sometimes. All those bastards should have been killed."

Conrad's new surprise was only that he didn't shoot Harry right then and there. The "he had it comin'" defense never looked saner. However, something inside him kept saying Harry possessed some knowledge of Hank's Heaven that killing him would destroy forever. The dormant academician's curiosity in him kicked in and kept him from pulling the trigger. Instead of a firearms shootout, he opted for verbal jousting.

"They were here long before any of us, and one thing I've learned in 15 months is they deserve to be here as much as we do...and I prefer their company to humans."

"You sound just like my brother."

"Thank you."

"Didn't mean it as a damned compliment. He was always too nice to these mother------- beasts, and damned if we didn't all pay for it sometimes. You bleedin' heart bastards never learn and just trade your softness about people to softness about animals. Hell, all God's creatures are the same – some good, some bad, and some just need killin'. And you...you were always so f------ polite – never trusted polite people. They'd just as soon shoot you in the back."

"I'm not going to argue with that, because it might be the first thing you've ever said I can even partially agree with. But understand that I prefer to shoot you point blank in front of you, but there is one way I would shoot you in the back."

"Yeah, what's that, boy?"

"If your back was toward me."

Harry laughed out loud, the first time Conrad ever heard the laugh.

"Dammit to hell, you're all right, boy. And you can shoot me if you want. I'm 90 years old today and figure to go out in a blaze of glory. I can't tell you how pissed I am at how this f----- country treats us old folks. All they want to do is put us out to pasture and let us die of cancer or the crazies or something else that whatever f----- old folks home you're in can take yours and the gummit's money. That shit ain't for me. Go ahead and shoot me boy. I came here to die and, if you're the man I been followin' in the papers, you got to shoot me. C'mon, 'Trespasser Killer', shoot me right between the eyes and put this old f----- out of his misery."

"Why didn't you open the door and let the big cat do it? He wanted you bad."

"Not goin' that way – not goin' to let a damned critter kill me – no way for a man of my life to go. No, a shootout is the way to go, western-style. C'mon, boy, let's walk out the paces and do this thing."

With that, the old man limped, like Walter Brennan in a John Wayne movie, a short distance down the path. Turning back to the cabin and to Conrad, Harry seemed amused.

"Damned liar – my back was to you – missed your chance, boy. Now put up or shut up."

Conrad, tired of the term boy anyway, decided to play along with this old man's request. A shot of adrenaline surged through him. Killing this man would probably get him some favor from his departed relatives, who at one time had all talked about putting Harry six feet under.

He also thought it might win him some more points with Gallaraga, never a bad thing. Conrad walked into the path and stood about twenty feet away.

"All right, boy, time to get it on. How do you want to do this? Count to three? Just go for it? Your place, your rules."

"We'll do the one, two, three, but if you want me to go through with this, I need to have a couple of questions answered first."

"Time's a wastin', boy, but if I can, I'll give you answers."

"Why did The Big Cat want to kill you?"

"He's a damned vicious animal."

"No, he's not. I've been around him too long. He doesn't attack for no reason and that's the first time I've ever seen him mad."

"Maybe he doesn't like loud-ass pickup trucks."

"I'm going to shoot you in the leg and let you suffer if you don't answer my question. Why did Gallaraga want you dead?"

"Gallaraga? Oh…the big cat…that's right damned original, boy. I remember that ballplayer – helluva hitter and a solid first baseman."

Conrad drew his gun with lightning speed, which let the old man know this was not going to be a match he could win. But Conrad didn't want to shoot…yet.

"One more time: why did Gallaraga want you dead?"

"None of your f------ business, boy. Now holster that weapon and let's do this for keeps."

For some reason unknown to him, Conrad complied. The old man showed surprise.

"I was born in the wrong century, boy. Should have been an outlaw in the old west. That would have suited me. Could have been a lawman, too, like Wyatt Earp or Seth Bullock – they were outlaws and lawmen – best of both worlds. This century was too damned civilized for me – too many motherf------ always wanting something and not caring about anyone but themselves. I will say this: Hank was the best person I ever knew, and I hated him for it. I tell you, boy, your Grandfather was the second-best man I ever knew, and I hated him too. You remind me some of him, and don't you go thankin' me for that."

"Thank you."

"Sumbitch!" but the smile betrayed Harry, who seemed happy with himself. Conrad wondered if this was a first.

"Are you ready, Harry...anything else to say?"

"I have a lot to say but nobody ever wanted to hear it? I'm taking my stories to the grave, boy. Let's do it."

"Here we go...one......two......three!"

Conrad pulled his gun and hesitated for just a moment to allow Harry to get his gun out of the holster. The moment that happened, Conrad fired.

Harry fell to his knees and looked contemptuously at his assailant, whose gun smoked and remained pointed at the heart of the old man.

"You shot my f------ hand, you bastard. That's nowhere near my heart, you asshole!"

"Your hand was toward me."

Chapter 30...100 Proof Conversation

"Now we're going to talk or I'm going to put you through torture not even you deserve."

"I hate you, you sumbitch."

"That makes me part of a big club. Now let's go inside and fix up that hand."

The two men walked inside, with the younger helping the older, who struggled to even make the slight step up into the cabin. He walked him to his other, older rocking chair, one familiar to the injured Harry.

"You still got this old thing? Hell, it's older than me. Did you shoot this thing too?"

A small hole was visible in the antique.

"No, I'm just not good at manual labor, and I put that hole in it when upholstering the chair. Just left it that way – wasn't planning on ever having anyone sit in it besides me."

"Guess I ought to consider it a f------ honor, huh?"

"It's only an honor that you're still alive for the moment, but that's only because I'm going to find out a few things about this place, and you're the only person who might know."

Conrad treated Harry's hand, finishing with a bandaging any nurse would be proud to call their work. During the treatment, Harry's demeanor changed from hatred to...non-hatred. Conrad figured that was about as far as Harry could go toward getting along with someone – especially someone who quite recently put a bullet through him.

As Conrad admired his handiwork, his guest rocked slowly, then leaned forward.

"So, you're not going to offer me anything to try to suck up to me for story hour? Dammit to hell, it's five o'clock somewhere."

"Getting close to five o'clock here. Want some tea, soda, or a beer? I've got a few Heineken cold."

"Don't you have anything real men drink? Hank and I used to make a mean moonshine here – bet you didn't know that, did you, boy?"

"No, I didn't, but I know my Grandmother made her own home brew – beer, not bourbon. Me, I'm not a beer drinker – never cultivated a taste for it, but I have one once in a while on those summer days when thirst just not going to be quenched by soda or Gatorade. I guess you'd be interested in a shot or three of bourbon."

"Damned straight, and that's how I want it – damned straight in the glass."

Conrad went to the cabinet and opened the door to one of his pride and joy possessions: an extensive shotglass collection. His life story could almost be told through the various one and two-ounce containers in front of him. He was especially proud of his college section: Western Kentucky with the big red towel, Louisville Cardinals, University of South Florida, University of Central Florida, and the two represented most – University of Kentucky and Notre Dame. Over the years, when people gave him gifts, those knowing him best gave him shotglasses. He ascertained the UK and ND glasses were easiest to come by – those fans drank more than other schools.

Chuckling at his joke, he opened the liquor cabinet and decided for himself on his favorite, then asked his guest about preferences.

"The stronger, the better, boy, if it ain't at least 100 proof, might as well drink cough syrup."

A strange feeling came over Conrad as he remembered that saying being a standard of his Father's – one he'd heard time and time again growing up. It was one of the main reasons he drank Knob Creek Bourbon – 100 proof. He kept a bottle of Booker's, 129 proof, on hand for special occasions, but this, as of yet, didn't rank in that category.

"Knob Creek is my choice of bourbons, Harry, so is that amenable?"

"Hell yes, and cut out those big words, boy, you ain't in the classroom anymore and I ain't your student. Pour the shot and bring it here…and bring the damned bottle with you."

Conrad poured the shots, tucked the pint bottle under his arm, and walked back into the living room. Placing each on the tv tray, he then handed the University of Louisville shotglass to Harry while keeping his favorite Tampa Bay Rays' glass for himself.

"U of Hell – great school, boy. You know, I went there for a couple of semesters."

"No, I didn't. My Dad went there and played baseball for the Cardinals."

"Yeah, I know. Your Dad was a good man. Don't know why he married into that family, but I guess he had his reasons."

Typical Harry – even when he said something nice, there was always the dig to get under someone's skin.

"How come you didn't stay?"

"The powers that be decided I was not college material. One day the dean of student affairs called me in and told me the army would be good for me. Wound up staring at the Krauts in Normandy – damnedest thing I ever went through. Nasty shit. None of us were ever quite right after those days. You sonbitches never appreciated what we did so you can have your so-called isolation freedom."

"Stop...no generation in history was ever more honored as yours, and I'm not saying you didn't deserve it. But the martyr syndrome doesn't play well. It wasn't like you had a big choice in the matter. You were drafted and told where to go. I know that opinion's not politically correct and would get me villainized if said in public, but it's the truth. I thank all of you guys for what you did, but sacrifice comes when you don't have to do something. The current generation of soldiers are the heroes – there's no draft – these people enlisted knowing we were at war and they would probably be sent into battle. They are the true sacrificers."

"What do you know about it? You never were a soldier, were you?"

"No, but I praise and celebrate the military at every opportunity. Don't get me wrong, even if one is forced into it, one still has to serve. I don't mean to diss your generation, and you did your duty, but again, there weren't a lot of choices in that matter."

Conrad handed the shot and asked his guest to make the first toast.

"Well, let's drink to those who went before us, most of 'em I'm damned glad are gone."

Shaking his head, Conrad joined Harry in downing the shot of 100 proof bourbon. The small kick associated with the esophagus and stomach were welcome additions to his system.

"Don't be chintzy, boy, pour me another one. If you're trying to get me drunk and get me to spill my guts, you need a helluva lot more than one drink."

"How many will it take?"

"We'll be here awhile."

Time for the second toast, also given by Harry.

"Here's to my brother Hank, who built this place we're on and did a helluva job…"

Conrad's heart warmed a bit to see a positive side of Harry, but reality quickly reared its ugly head.

"…may the sumbitch rot in hell for not leaving the place to me!"

The bitter tone of Harry's words struck Conrad as understanding grew of who this man truly was. With a third shot poured, Conrad put a different spin in an attempt to be positive.

"I always make the third toast the same, Harry. I got it from one of my favorite movies, *Gardens of Stone*, with James Earl Jones, James Caan and Anjelica Huston. They always toasted the same way and my third toast echoes theirs."

Harry actually brightened some and indicated he knew the toast as well. The two said in unison: "Here's to us and those like us…damned few left!"

Both sat back in their respective places, pondering the toasts and those who went before them.

"Harry, that's it for me. Three shots are my limit. I normally only have two shots three times a week – the healthy way to drink. So I'm done drinking. I'll pour you as many as you want."

"So you are a big wuss, huh? Thought so, but you do whatever works; as for me, keep pouring until I pass out, then pour one after that."

Conrad put out a tray of snacks to help soak up the alcohol, and eight additional shots later, stared at his great uncle (no blood relation) with admiration and contempt. Harry saw both.

"I know you don't like me, boy, nobody does, and I don't give a rat's ass in hell what they think about me. Hell, that makes you and me a lot alike, boy – the only difference is you kicked everybody out at your age and I'm still living on someone else's dime. Damned degrading the way my life is, boy. I came here for you to be a man of your word. I'm trespassing, and if you're the honest sumbitch you say you are, then you'll put a bullet between my eyes and end this f------ misery. I've lived with lies and secrets long enough, and it's my time to go and meet the damned devil. I'm gonna kick his ass when I see him."

Harry smiled a drunken smile and tried to get out of the chair, but he might as well have been shackled to it. Resigned to stay there, he let out a belch that nearly shook the room.

"I'd say excuse me, but there's no excuse for me."

"Had enough to tell me your tale, Harry?...Harry?...DAMMIT HARRY!"

The old man celebrated the end of his 90th birthday by passing out in the rocking chair in the cabin at Hank's Heaven. Part of Conrad was glad he allowed the man this day that seemed to have ended on a somewhat happy note. However, a question that plagued him caused a battle within himself. He thought of all possibilities, pro and con, and believed the right decision was forthcoming.

Conrad stood, facing Harry. He unholstered the glock and pointed it directly between the eyes of his great uncle (no blood relation). While he knew where to find sympathy in the dictionary, he couldn't shake the feeling that putting this man out of his miserable existence was the right thing, not just for the man, but for all of humanity. The other side of the coin was acquiescing to what this man wanted – so many people are not afforded the opportunity to go out of this life on their terms, why should this miserable excuse for a person?

Certainty needed, he ran through the options again, and in the final analysis, believed life was inevitably unfair so killing him on his own terms was incredibly unfair to humanity...that's the way it should be. He recited "The Serenity Prayer" once again, and asked God for a sign if he was doing the right thing.

At that moment, a roar rang through the cabin. It was 10:00 p.m., but Gallaraga was not ready for the evening routine. Something else was on his mind.

Conrad put the gun down and looked at the sleeping excrement, unfazed by the big cat's call.

Chapter 31...If the Cat's Got Your Tongue, Give it Booker's

Making sure all guns were hidden, Conrad left Harry alone and went into the bedroom, locking the door behind him. He went to the window and, instead of Gallaraga perched facing the small pond (which needed a name), was met by the big cat's face directly in the window. Conrad felt certain Gallaraga was trying to communicate something, perhaps to let him in, perhaps to let Harry out, but whatever, it would keep another day. The story wanted remained untold, and no killing would take place until the storytelling occurred.

"Not tonight, big boy...I'm going to ask you what I've asked of creatures before...give me 24 hours to find out what I want to find out. Then, we'll go from there. But for tonight, nothing is going to happen."

Conrad pointed to the hay bed, but this time, Gallaraga did not obey. He walked across the dam, bounded halfway up the hillside, and let out the now-familiar roar of disapproval. Peering with a touch of sadness out the window at his friend, Conrad hoped the big cat would forgive him for putting off the killing of Harry. He further hoped the relationship was undamaged.

The next morning, Conrad found Harry unmoved from the rocking chair. Bacon and eggs frying woke the old man, and no hangover seemed present. Drinking abusively and passing out in a chair were things familiar to Harry, and perhaps gave an explanation as to his nasty attitude.

"I hope you're making enough for both of us, boy. I'd hate to eat alone."

Putting the food and a hot cup of coffee in front of the old man, Conrad didn't know how to feel about himself. Was he breaking his own code by not simply shooting this person? Could one trespass on a place that was his immediate family's for so many years? Why did Gallaraga feel so much animosity toward this man? The big cat never returned overnight, which worried Conrad, but not a great deal – nothing other than humans for Gallaraga to fear, and there were only two humans on the property.

"Not bad. You make a good wife."

"My guess is you are still trying to goad me into shooting you between the eyes."

"I wasn't expecting to wake up this morning. Last night was a great way to go and I'm damned pissed you didn't shoot me."

"Not going to shoot you in the cabin, Harry, then I'd have to clean up the blood. If and when I shoot you, it will be outside where it all washes down the hillsides. But I'll tell you what...you tell me the story I want to know, and I'll make sure you never leave here alive."

"I'll think about it, now how about another couple of strips of bacon?"

"All right, but remember, I'm not your slave...and you will tell me the story."

"So, I can rest assured this is my last day?"

"We can say that...as long as you hold up your end of the bargain."

"Deal...shake on it. My word is my bond."

The two men shook hands, and after the dishes were put away, Conrad decided to leave the old man alone. He emptied the barrels of all guns except the glock and the dresser drawer revolver, and put the shells in a locked cabinet, placing the only cabinet key in his pocket. He wasn't going far, anyway, simply checking on the animals at the A-frame.

To his surprise, no animals dined that day. Even Mama Kitty was nowhere to be found, and the kittens who were now cats themselves were out of sight. No birds, no Pewie, no Beasman...nobody. The A-frame yard, which teemed with wildlife every morning, appeared a veritable ghost town.

I guess they don't like Harry either.

He called out the names of the various critters, but none answered. Only slightly puzzled, he decided to deviate from the usual pattern of sitting in the lounge chair. A walk back to the cabin saw Harry sitting outside in Conrad's favorite rocking chair. The old man showed no ill effects of the previous night, having moved the chair to the small pond's edge, back to the cabin. Gallaraga remained nowhere to be found, and Conrad mused this would have been a golden opportunity for an attack.

The old boy must've listened to me last night and given me 24 hours.

Pulling his glock just in case the old man found something he'd overlooked, Conrad walked beside the rocker. Harry appeared deep in thought and further appeared troubled by those thoughts. Silence ensued for quite some time, with the only break coming with an inquisition into whether or not Harry wanted to try his luck fishing.

He did not. Fishing was never his thing.

"Gigantic waste of f------ time, if you ask me."

Desire to shoot the man returned. Harry's reputation for pissing people off was well earned – he always knew the proper buttons to push.

"How was the menagerie, Ellie Mae?"

"Nobody home, Jethrine. They apparently knew you were here and all went on vacation. Can't say as I blame them. You are a nasty old sumbitch, aren't you?"

"Always have been. I think the only person I ever got along with was Hank, and I don't think he liked me either. Hell, you know your Grandfather beat the shit out of me one time here on the farm."

"Yeah, it seemed to be everyone's favorite day – the day Harry got his comeuppance."

"I started to kill that old fart, but hell, I mouthed off and he shut it. Can't really hold him responsible for something's that was my fault. He told me to shut up and I didn't, and I probably shouldn't have made a pass at that cute little filly that was your Grandma."

"Oh, I think you could have said anything to him – called him anything in the book, and he'd been okay, but trying to mess with her was something no one did. I'm surprised he didn't kill you."

"Would have, if Hank hadn't stopped him. I was surprised Hank did, and it took Hank and Pete to pull that big f----- off me."

"I liked Pete."

Silence resumed, but this time an uncomfortable silence. The name of the younger brother being spoken caused a sweeping feeling through Harry on which Conrad couldn't quite put a finger. Whatever the feeling was, negative dominated. A lone tear streamed down the old man's face.

Guilt...that's the feeling...Harry feels guilt about something concerning Pete.

The evening could no longer come soon enough. Conrad tried to keep busy by calling up his usual online sites. Not much of interest this day – even Yahoo News produced little of interest, other than yet another professional athlete in trouble over domestic violence. The only twist this day was the fact a woman beat a football player with a baseball bat instead of the other way around. His affair with a basketball player caused the beating and Conrad raised his eyebrow Spock-like after reading the other player's league was not the WNBA, but the NBA – an interesting twist.

Lunch was the standard p b and j sandwiches, and Harry gladly accepted, demanding milk and chastising anyone who would drink anything but milk with peanut butter and jelly.

"Communistic to not drink milk with these sandwiches, and I hate those commie bastards."

Conrad drank his Pepsi with increased pride at urinating Harry off for a change.

The guest went back to the chair, asserting he took a nap every afternoon at this time. Conrad felt comfortable staying on routine, although locking the bedroom door as a precaution. His slumber was disturbed by knocking at the door.

"Happy Hour, you young whipper-snapper. Don't sleep your life away! Get your ass up and let's have some more shots."

Three shots produced the same toasts as the night before along with meaningless conversation regarding the nature of mankind and the nature of nature. Harry rambled on about nothing in particular until it was time for dinner. Conrad fried burgers on the George Foreman grill and added baked beans to the plate.

"Where the hell is the big onion, boy? You can't have a f------ cheeseburger in paradise without a big-ass onion!"

Conrad complied and sliced an onion onto a plate placed on the tv tray in front of the rocking chair.

"Now you're talkin'. This is my favorite meal, boy – I've lived 90 years on cheeseburgers and baked beans."

"What do your doctors say?"

"My doctors are all dead. Ya know, I never had a doctor didn't smoke like a f------ chimney and take too much of their own medicines, if you know what I mean. They were always about three sheets in the wind. Now they're asses are dead and I'm 90 years old. F--- 'em all!"

He attacked the meal like it was his last, savoring every bite. With each bite of burger, he would take a bite of a sliced onion, then a spoonful of beans, then a drink of Pepsi, the drink demanded at supper.

Conrad hoped the several similarities witnessed that day between the two of them were the only similarities. He still detested this man, still wanted to kill him, but still wanted to know the man's story.

Dinner completed, Harry demanded more bourbon. Conrad decided the old man drank enough of the good stuff, and poured a shot of Evan Williams instead. The 86 proof product was a gift from an old friend who worked at Heaven Hill for 32 years and could not bring himself to give his old friend his favored Jim Beam product. To be fair, even though he felt no need for fairness, Conrad poured himself the same bourbon.

"Got a toast, Harry?"

"Here's to my host, the 'Trespasser Killer', may my death never cause you a moment's regret."

"I will definitely drink to that."

Both men threw the shots down, but Harry's face turned ugly first.

"Godd-----, boy! I'm not good enough for the good stuff on my last night! This is that Heaven Hill shit, and it's not even their best brand...this 86 proof crap is for wimps and little girls. Get me the 100 proof or shoot me right now."

"I'm impressed, Harry, and it's hard to impress me. I thought my father was the only man who possessed that talented a set of taste buds. He could tell you brand and proof as well, but if you noticed, I'm drinking the same as you. Tell you what, I'll make it up to us and get out the good stuff I've been saving."

"Booker's?"

"Booker's!"

Retrieving the bottle of what he considered the best bourbon in the world, Conrad took his time opening the bottle of Booker's, remembering two of the best men he'd known: Booker Noe and his son, Fred Booker Noe. Loud, large and gregarious, they represented their business with color and flair difficult to match in this day and age, and he remembered their kindness regarding his Hemingway shows – often sending him a bottle or three before a big tour. In his shows, their friendship was always mentioned.

Booker's opened, the air changed as the 129 proof took over. Shots poured, Conrad quickly made known this toast was his.

"To Booker and Fred Noe, one who lived long and prospered, and the other who lived strong and, at last check, was still prospering."

Harry couldn't care less about the toast, too happy about getting a chance to imbibe the best. On his limited social security income, Booker's was a brand unaffordable. He savored the shot a bit more, sipping rather than gulping the product. His drinking partner followed suit.

They poured another but no toast ensued. Instead, Conrad insisted on the promise being fulfilled. Harry nodded, but pointed to his empty glass, giving the message that a third shot would be consumed before storytelling commenced. The third shot poured and drunk, the old man sat back in the rocking chair, breathed a bit heavier than normal, looked his partner directly in the eye, and began the tale.

Chapter 32...A Tale of Three Brothers

"I would start out by sayin' anyone hearin' my tale would probably end up not liking me, but hell, since no one likes me anyway, that's not a problem. I lived my life my way by my rules and I don't have one single f------ regret. 'Cept maybe how I treated my daughter, but that's not part of this story, so to hell with that. I'm guessin' the part of the story you want is why that damned cat of yours wants to eat me alive, am I right?"

"That's right, Harry, he obviously has it in for you, but I've run him off for the time being. I expect he'll be back."

"I expect so, and I 'spect he's a cub of this one panther I had a run-in with a long time ago. Hated that cat. He was always comin' 'round and sitting around when Hank was here. You probably never saw him 'cause he made himself scarce whenever civilized folks were around. Guess he didn't think I was civilized and he was probably right, and he growled at me every time I came to see Hank. Hank and I would drink some moonshine, tell lies based on the truth, and drink some more.

Well, you know Pete stayed out here a lot of the time because he wasn't no good for anything else except keepin' Hank company, so Hank, bein' the good-hearted soul I ain't, let Pete stay in this cabin. Hank used to tell the story that this one big-ass cat would actually wait for Pete to go to sleep at night and then bed down right next to the cabin by the pond. I saw you got some hay in the spot where Hank says this here cat liked to sleep. I never believed him – sounded like one of my brother's tall tales he liked to spin. Them cats ain't good for nuthin' but shootin', and I always wanted to shoot that cat and threatened to do it on a couple of occasions – 'specially when I'd had a bit too much shine. Hank always stopped me, but a couple of times I shot my gun up in the air to scare the shit out of the critter – he'd run away and not come back for a while. I thought it was funny, but Pete would get pissed every time I'd do it. You know, he hardly ever got mad and wouldn't hurt a fly – them type of people seem to be that way – but he was strange when it came to that cat. It was like they were mates or some sick shit like that, but Hank said they hung around together a lot. Stupid shit, you know animals will turn on you anytime. I had a dog when I was a young'un that turned on me. I took a bone from it one day and it bit the hell outta me. So I shot the sonofabitch and ain't liked animals since."

Conrad reached and poured another shot of the Booker's into the Louisville Cardinals shotglass. The storyteller nodded his head in approval and raised his glass with a bit of sorry on his face.

"Here's to Brother Pete...dumbass to the end."

The bourbon consumed, Harry hesitated a moment, rocked back into his chair, and continued.

"You do know that this land is stolen land, don't you?"

"No, I got everything legalized and there's nothing wrong with my deed."

"I don't doubt it, but legal don't mean true, son."

Conrad noticed a change of tone, calling him "son" rather than "boy" for the first time in any conversation. He realized Harry didn't doubt the legality of anything, but there was another story inside the story.

"When Hank went to buy this property, he asked me if I wanted to go in on it, and I thought it would be a good investment. Lots of things die or rot or just go to hell, but there's always property. I figured we'd keep it for a few years and then sell it to some real estate developer and make a fortune.

But the one thing Hank insisted on was bringing in Pete on the deal. The three brothers in a partnership – that's what Hank wanted. But he wanted it equal and I didn't think Pete had any money. Came to find out later that Hank put up Pete's share and we formed what they call one of them LLCs – Limited Liability Corporations or whatever bullshit legal crap that is. What I didn't realize was those two bastards were in cahoots and started outvotin' me two to one on every damned thing. I couldn't get anything done. I wanted to build a big old mansion on that hill overlookin' the bigger pond – damn, that would have been a perty site. I was gonna run electric and city water but Hank would have none of it, and Pete wouldn't vote with Hank no matter what. So I stepped back for a bit and hoped things went to hell."

Frustration crossed Harry's face as he recalled the events. Conrad wondered how close to the truth this all was. There were rumors in the family that Hank once upon a time didn't own the place outright, but his name was the only one on the deed. If the brothers had a partnership, two of them were silent, but that wasn't all that unusual back in the day. Hank always seemed in charge and seldom mentioned Harry, but as Conrad recalled conversations between Hank and Grandfather, he realized Hank grimaced any time Harry's name was mentioned. Harry seemed to be the only human on the planet Hank didn't like, and that spoke volumes to Conrad. Maybe they both possessed reasons to dislike the other.

"Well, they didn't go to hell and he got the place just the way he liked it. He didn't want to spoil it at all, and I wanted to spoil it a little with a big house over the nicest lake. Shit, I wasn't askin' much, and I owned a third. Son, always get everything on paper, even if it's family. Hell, 'specially if it's family.

Anyways, I came out one day and was drinkin' shine with Hank at the A-frame when Pete comes down in one of those moods them people get into when they get agitated. He was mad 'cause someone shot one of the deer and accused me of doin' it. Well, for once I was innocent and told him so, but he didn't believe me. We got into a helluva argument and finally Hank told Pete to go on and cool off and leave me alone. Pete mumbled he was going over to the other pond and rest a spell.

Only time Hank ever took up for me, but I think he figured he was savin' Pete by getting him outta there. I was pissed and thought about shootin' him, and then it hit me: shootin' Pete would equal the partnership between me and Hank. If Pete was dead, his half went to the both of us, so me and Hank would then be on equal footin'. He was a simpleton with no future anyway, so what was the loss to anybody. The older Pete got, the dumber he got and the more burden he was, so killin' him would be doin' everybody a favor – even Hank, though I knew Hank wouldn't see it that way. Always protectin' little brother."

The storyteller paused and inhaled deeply, sitting back in the rocking chair and working to recall the timeline properly. Conrad took the break in the tale to pour himself another Booker's shot, filling the Notre Dame shotglass to the brim.

"Sounds like you made a bad choice. So you –"

"Shut the f--- up and let me finish, son; don't interrupt your elder. But you're damned right, I made a choice – whether it was bad or not depends upon how you look at it. I said goodbye to Hank and instead of goin' home, I went over to the pond. I didn't drive all the way there because I didn't want him to hear my pickup and run away. Didn't want him goin' anywhere. The old truck wasn't as loud as it used to be back in the day – it was a helluva vehicle and I ain't never got rid of it.

I was pretty good in the woods back in them days, so I snuck around the bottom of the dam and came up around Pete without him hearin'. He was just sittin' there on that damned bench like he didn't have a care in the world – hell, he never did and that just drove me crazy. But I wasn't goin' to shoot him in the back – ain't the manly thing to do and you know my opinion on that already. So I told him to stand up and face me. He did and seemed surprised to see a double-barrel shotgun staring at him. It was about then that damned cat jumped in front of Pete and started growling at me. Dumbass cat. He should've jumped me if he had any sense – as quick as the bastard was, I couldn't have done nothing, but now I could 'cause the cat was in front of me.

The stupid-ass critter raised up on his haunches like it was threatenin' me, so I let both barrels go. Both the cat and Pete went back into the water and I went back and made up a damned fine story to Hank about the cat trying to attack me and me shootin' it to save myself and I thought the shells went through the cat and killed Pete as well. We went back over there and Hank said the best thing to do is just leave 'em be. The turtles would get 'em and drag 'em to the bottom of the lake and nobody would ever know. But he'd keep his mouth shut on one condition: I leave there and never come back – leave him and the property alone. Somethin' about shootin' and killin', son, that you probably learned when you shot them people. It don't leave you happy. I ain't never gotten over it."

Conrad took a moment to take in the story and reflect for another moment.

"So, my finding the bodies screwed things up somewhat."

"Yeah, Hank figured they'd be gone by then, but the damned turtles left them alone and they just rotted 'till you found 'em. Rural cops at that time didn't know shit from shinola, and since it looked like a damned huntin' accident anyway, didn't want to waste their time and budget on the thing, so it all went away."

"Helluva story, Harry."

"One more drink and I'll wrap this up with one them Paul Harvey 'Rest of the Story" stories."

Intrigued, Conrad poured another shot of Booker's into the old man's glass. Harry took it, once again savored it, and even gargled it a bit before swallowing.

"Damned fine bourbon. Old Booker knew what the hell he was doin'."

Once again, he sat back in the rocker and returned to storytelling mode.

"I didn't tell you one thing that needs to be told. After I shot the cat and Pete, I heard some little meows from up the hill. When I looked up, there were two cubs looking like they wanted to attack me but were scaredy cats at that point. I took my gun and shot, but missed 'em. They took off up the hill. I'm guessin' one of them is your Gallaraga, or at least the pup of one of those two pups or, shit, maybe the grandpup of one of those pups. He don't look old enough to be one of them pups. Guess hatred gets passed down generations in animals and humans.

Conrad, my son, that's my story. I killed my own brother and have lived a long time with my secret. I don't regret it – put the bastard out of his misery and Hank's responsibility. Hank should have thanked me, but instead he took this property. F------ thief!"

"The story explains a great deal. I'm going to think a moment on it and take it all in."

"You promised I'd be dead before the end of the day if'n I told the story. Well, son, I told the story, and I expect you to live up to your end of the bargain."

"That I know is going to happen, but let me reflect on how to do this. Might walk over to the Big Lake and put a bullet in you in the same place as where you shot the cat and Pete. Remember, I'm an old lit professor and believe in the power of irony."

"I don't give a damn how you do it, just do it quick whenever the time comes."

Conrad looked at his cellphone: 9:55. An interesting concept crossed his brain, and he walked into his bedroom, hoping Gallaraga would come into view at 10:00 – the 24-hour timeframe they seemingly agreed upon.

Precisely at 10:00, a shadow appeared on the dam, but this shadow was not alone. Another shadow, about the same size, followed. As the shadows closed on the cabin, Conrad saw two big cats. Gallaraga's companion struggled a bit to maneuver across the dam, and soon came into full view at the window of the cabin. No roar…not even a growl. Conrad realized the second cat was much older than Gallaraga, and the interesting concept that crossed Conrad's brain earlier became clearer and increased in validation. He put up his hand to Gallaraga and went back into the living room where the old man sat.

"I've made my decision, Harry. C'mon, let's go."

"Son, I like the idea of going over to the other lake. Ashes to ashes, dust to dust, and that will be a good place to die."

As they walked out the door of the cabin, Conrad turned and walked back inside, locking the door behind him.

That night, Gallaraga and his family enjoyed justice.

Conrad buried what was left of Harry on the hillside a few feet below Pete and his Big Cat.

Harry deserved to be below.

Chapter 33...Endings and Beginnings

For the next year, Conrad Nevitt lived in the calmness and serenity envisioned when first moving to Hank's Heaven. Every day treasured, every day filled with planned serendipity, every day another day left to himself and the menagerie. They all returned shortly after Harry's burial, and Conrad found himself visiting the three gravesites as part of a twice a week walk with Gallaraga up the hillside.

Each time, one sight stood out: varying animal excrement on Harry's grave. It appeared the animals took turns defecating on the old man, and Conrad wondered if he should add to the decorations, but preferred not to, recalling the ending scene to the movie *Carrie* and not wanting Harry's dead hand to grab the particular part of Conrad that would be exposed. So he left the desecration to Joe Beasman and company. He wondered what vegetation would grow when spring appeared. Just past his 64th birthday, Conrad received his answer, as the ugliest weeds known to man and God began to sprout.

Poetic justice.

Winter once again begat spring which begat summer, and each day brought more joy to the retired professor. His daily journaling took on a more positive tone as he penned various fiction and nonfiction pieces, always based on either himself or things he knew. Hemingway's influence was never far away, but he adored the Faulkner style of letting the story take you where it wants to go. Combined with a degree of Angelou-style memoir and Sexton-style confessionalism, the time he spent writing became nearly as important as the time he spent with his new besties/beasties.

No one bothered him from the outside world. Thoughts that someone from Harry's family might come looking entered his mind but were now fleeting with the passage of time. The old man didn't own anything but the pickup truck, and he would gladly hand it over should any relative appear, unless they trespassed, and then, of course, they would die. He never worried about telling the story of Harry's death or worried about failure to report the death to authorities – if they wanted to know, he'd gladly tell them. The pickup truck stood idly by the barn near The Big Lake, where Conrad moved the vehicle shortly after Harry's death. A bit of an eyesore, he surmised it was now a useful tool, providing shelter to whatever animal deemed to call it home. It made a great place to hide from predators and raise little critters.

The Fourth of July came and passed, with particular celebration for Conrad, given the success of the quest for freedom and independence. This year, he barbecued on the old pit of Hank's, flipping small chunks of burger and hot dog to any of the creatures who wandered into the pit area to see what the master chef had on the grill. Bits of bun were fed to the birds, highlighted by the re-appearance of the blue heron. He alit on top of the barbecue pit, as if to announce his presence and critique the chef. Always a bird that thought he ran whatever show he was in, he chased the other birds away, and received a chastising from Conrad. The bird seemed to realize his error, and when the birds returned a third time, as persistent birds do, the heron left them alone and was treated to both burger and bun. Conrad strategically place some burger bit and bun bit so that, when the heron ate, Conrad could inspect the area under the wing to see if this bird was indeed Scotty. He thought about how far-fetched the idea was, but these things kept him amused.

As blue herons do often before feeding, the heron expanded his wings outward to ward off anyone trying to steal a free meal from the freeloader. When he did, the scar under the wing became visible to Conrad. Indeed, it was Scott, and when Conrad called his name, the bird squawked in reply. With that, a larger burger bit and bun was placed in front of the bird, who enjoyed no fear with his former Florida friend. The reunion was complete. Scotty would stay until time to head south for the winter.

Although most in his family enjoyed all the festivities surrounding the Fourth of July, fireworks were never part of him, and none were set off on the property, although he could hear them in the distance emanating from the small towns miles away. The animals, except for Pewie, seemed oblivious, but Pewie ran back and forth nervously before heading back up the path to just above the cabin where he and his family established residency.

"Scaredy polecat!"

Pewie, as usual, paid no mind to his friend and, with his companion and the young'uns, sped in single-line formation to their home.

The meal finished and cleanup completed, Conrad headed to his home as well. Sitting back on the couch, he turned on the baseball games and shook his head at all the red, white and blue caps designed specifically for this day.

If I thought it was for patriotism, I would love these hats…but with MLB, it's all about making money and selling a bunch of specialty hats. They should all be green and have thousand dollar bills as the logo. Always follow the money.

He thought of Arturo and his family. The last few e-mails unanswered, which was not all that unusual to go some degree of time between communications, bothered Conrad a bit more this time. Reading the latest stories from Yahoo News gave no indication of any bad events among any of the crime families, and he knew bad things happening to organized crime figures normally made headlines across the world. Still, he felt an uneasiness that his communications failed to elicit responses.

After bidding Gallaraga goodnight, Conrad was about to lie down when the laptop bing signaled a message. Normally, the message would be left until the next morning, but hoping Arte responded, Conrad opened the messages.

Dear Mr. Nevitt,

As per your request, I'm continuing my every six months' request to write your memoirs. It's been six months since the last time I asked, so I'm asking on your timeline. As always, I promise to do the best job possible to tell the story you want told. I look forward to the time when you give me a positive response so we can sit down together and enjoy putting together your life story.

Sincerely,

Tom Howlett

Admiring the reporter's persistence, patience, and grammar, for the first time, Conrad seriously considered the request. Perhaps the time had come to tell the story and let this young man obtain some published recognition. After all, he enjoyed reading Howlett's now daily column and trusted him nearly as much as he'd trusted Walter Cronkite and Jon Stewart. Since neither of them would write the tale, Howlett was the next best option.

He would sleep on it and if he continued positive, he would send a positive response.

The next morning, the pro-Howlett feelings remained, so he send an affirmative communication.

Dear Tom,

Thank you for your continued interest in this old man's story. I tell you what: let's do it! Come to the main gate of Hank's Heaven on August 12 at 4:00 and prepare to come back every day from 4-7 until the deed is done. We'll take weekends off. BYOP and TR: Bring your own pad and tape recorder. Let me know if this schedule is amenable to you and make sure you press the right button on the main gate when you come. I'd hate to shoot you accidentally.

Live long and prosper,

Conrad

The reporter responded with enthusiasm right away, and plans cemented. Over the next five weeks, Conrad gave great thought as to how he wanted his story told and jotted down some of the things he definitely wanted in the book. His outline comprised several pages, a far cry from Charles Dickens' elaborate outlines but much more organized than Capote or Faulkner. He performed his Truman Capote imitation for Gallaraga, but the big cat failed to even feign enthusiasm, simply rolling over on his back and letting out a snarl.

There's a critic in every crowd.

On August 12, precisely at 4:00, the gate monitor blinked on. Conrad called to the monitor there.

"Is there anyone there that needs shooting?"

"No sir, Mr. Nevitt, it's Tom Howlett, on time and ready to write."

"The gate will open shortly, Tom, c'mon up."

A couple of minutes later, Conrad, sitting in his old rocker in front of the cabin, greeted his biographer.

"Punctual – you know how much I like that. Come and sit a moment before we start. Would you like a cold beverage?"

"No thank you, sir, I brought my own if you don't mind."

The reporter took out a Miller High Life and opened it before sitting in the chair placed a few feet from his interviewee. Smiling, Conrad held up his Western Kentucky University shotglass and proposed a toast.

"Qapla'!"

"Qapla' to us both!"

"Do you speak Klingon, Tom?"

"No, sir."

"The word means 'success'. Listen, calling me sir is like putting a tuxedo on a goat – doesn't go together at this point. Call me Conrad and I'll call you Tom and we'll get along just fine."

He sensed nervousness in the reporter, but felt it go away a smidgeon after they hit glasses and downed their respective beverages. Conrad poured a second shot of 100 proof and lifted his glass for Tom to make the next toast.

"O.K., Conrad, here's to the life you've lived and getting it down properly in print."

Glasses touched again and the second toast completed.

"I've taken the time to jot down a few things that you can use as you like – it's sort of an outline with some specific quotations contained therein. Use it, burn it, or use it as illustrations in the middle of this thing – whatever you want to do."

"Thank you. I'm sure they'll be of good use. If you don't mind, what I'd like to do is turn the recorder on and merely talk. I'm thinking *Conversations with Conrad, The Trespasser Killer* would make a good title – with your permission of course."

"That's a pretty good working title. You know, I thought I was a poet at one point in my life...loved rhyming and not rhyming, onomatopoeia, metaphor and all that shit. At least the title's alliterative. I don't like the Killer thing in the title, but I guess it's appropriate and will help you sell books."

"If we come up with something better as we go along, we'll change it."

"Good deal. Now, Tom, what do you want to talk about first?"

"I guess we ought to start at the crux of this and work backwards, sideways and frontwards. What gave you the idea to isolate?"

Conrad poured a third shot into his WKU glass but put off drinking it as he reflected upon his answer. Then, he reached under his outdoor table and produced a magazine cover from *Harper's*, April 2015.

"I read an article in this magazine by author Fenton Johnson. The title is 'Going It Alone'. He writes about the dignity and challenge of solitude. After reading the article, I knew I wanted to try being by myself for the first time in my life and seeing if I liked it. His was about living alone and its beauties – I wanted to take a step further by taking humanity out of the equation altogether. I figured if it didn't work, I'd simply go back to the life with people around. The life of living for others, the one my parents and grandparents raised me on, jaded me to the point of no longer liking people – all the damned users who seek out the givers and take advantage of them. It's hard for the givers to see through the evil nature of the users – too busy giving to notice what's really happening.

Over the past two years, I've, for the most part, gotten away from everything. Had to establish my territory and did that successfully – had run-ins with people from time to time, but all that worked itself out and you're the first person on this property for quite a while. The good news for me is I don't miss people at all and that was a great worry. I once thought I was one of those do-gooders who always had to do good for others in order to be happy. Meanwhile, I was living my life for everyone but the one person who should matter to me: me. My grandmother once said, "I take care of me first, then I can take care of everyone else." I thought that was the most selfish thing ever came out of someone's mouth, but then realized what she meant. If you don't take care of yourself, you'll lose yourself and then won't be able to do a damned thing. But if you're happy, then it's easier to help others around you be happy. So I did my thing for a long time, but then, in the end, I did the thing to save my own existence and so far, it's been the best call I've ever made."

Tom Howlett changed crossed legs in his chair, and continued the line of questioning.

"Well, I guess the appropriate next question is, then, are you happy?"

"Damned fine question, my boy, because it proves you're listening. Old Mike Wallace would be proud of you for that – a good journalist listens and bases the next question on something picked up upon during the answer to the first question."

"Oh, no, Conrad, if I get too much like Mike Wallace, I know you'll shoot me!"

"True...most of his interviewees would have liked to take a mallet to him, I think, except Ayn Rand – she carved him up pretty well, but that was early in his career. He said he learned a lot from that interview. It's on YouTube, by the way, in case you ever want to see it."

"Are you happy, Conrad Nevitt?"

"Guess I need to figure out what happiness is first. I believe my definition of happiness to be a state of mind where contentment plus anticipation plus revelation keeps even an old man wide-eyed at what each moment brings. At 64, my level of anticipation for whatever's next is exceeded only by the revelation of all the good times past, present, and ahead. I am content within my own mind that what I've done, what I'm doing, and what I'm going to do are my choices to make and I'll make choices that suit my personality.

That's my bullshit answer.

My other, more concise answer, is you know it when you are and you can't really describe it."

The two men talked for three hours about, as the interviewee put it, things of the mind and the spirit. While the conversation seemed to lack direction and focus, the reporter never wavered from the non-path path of the discussion.

At 7:00, Conrad's cellphone beeped, signaling an end to the first day's discussion. He lifted his glass.

"Here's to us and those like us...damned few left."

The empty Miller bottle clanked with the full WKU glass, and Tom Howlett smiled and feigned a drink as Conrad Nevitt threw the third shot down. They stood, shook hands, and the reporter pledged to return the next day, hoping for as much productivity as the opener.

"Productivity still one of those buzz words in the profession?"

"Yes, sir, I mean, Conrad, yes it is."

"I'll see you tomorrow."

As Tom Howlett stepped toward his vehicle, the ringtone of "Camptown Races" signaled an incoming message from his boss. He checked the script and his face went tight.

"Conrad, I might not be able to make it tomorrow. My boss says to drop everything I'm doing for a story he needs me to cover."

Conrad didn't know whether to be mad, be sympathetic, or to shoot the reporter as all three thoughts raced equally through his head. His like of this reporter combined with the sad look on Howlett's face kept the glock holstered.

"What's going on? Perhaps we can put this off if it's a worthy story."

"My boss just texted that he needs me to cover a story about a local girl who's gone missing in Atlantic City."

Conrad's heart dropped and Tom realized the connection quickly.

"Oh, damn, Mr. Nevitt, it's Catherine Smith."

"Tell me what's happened."

"The text says that she and her parents, Mr. and Mrs. Arturo Palizzino, are reported missing and presumed dead after an attack on the family compound just outside of Atlantic City…"

The thought that Conrad was about to end his isolation began percolating.